ABOUT THE AUTHOR

Ph_____ ____ ιos

Ned Livingst_____ .ı South Africa and came
to England in the ɛ_____. He was amongst those who
protested against apa_..ıeid outside South Africa House
in Trafalgar Square.

He qualified as a Dental Surgeon in South Africa and
lived for some tome in Manchester, in Hampshire and in
London.

He trained as a pilot in South Africa. His hobbies
include art, music and current affairs.

During his time as a university student in Johannesburg, he and several of his friends were placed under sur-
veillance by the apartheid authorities. Some of his friends
went underground or mysteriously disappeared, never to
be seen again. Some were arrested. The father of one of his

friends active in the anti apartheid movement was shot and killed by unknown persons.

The anti apartheid counter intelligence movement attempted to recruit him into their service as an agent.

During his time in South Africa his practice was used as a drop address for secret correspondence for the anti apartheid movement from abroad. He fed the authorities snippets of information and false information aimed at misleading them.

The author's political convictions underwent a radical change, when after the ascension to power of the African National Congress, South Africa descended into near anarchy, crime and lawlessness.

The Xhosa Double

Ned Livingstone

iUniverse, Inc.
New York   Bloomington

The Xhosa Double

iUniverse books may be ordered through booksellers or by contacting:

iUniverse
1663 Liberty Drive
Bloomington, IN 47403
www.iuniverse.com
1-800-Authors (1-800-288-4677)

*Because of the dynamic nature of the Internet, any Web addresses or
links contained in this book may have changed since publication and may
no longer be valid. The views expressed in this work are solely those of
the author and do not necessarily reflect the views of the publisher, and
the publisher hereby disclaims any responsibility for them.*

ISBN: 978-1-4401-6939-7 (pbk)
ISBN: 978-1-4401-6940-3 (ebook)

Printed in the United States of America

iUniverse rev. date: 9/9/09

ACKNOWLEDGEMENT

My sincere thanks to David Kozman and Pat Sands-Anis for help and advice with the manuscript and to Monty Joffin and Dean Marks for help with formatting.

PREAMBLE.
1936.

Sipho, aged eighteen, lay in agony on the reed matt in the hut. Reaching under the none too clean cloth loosely wrapped around his lower waist, he touched his penis, or rather he touched the mud and blood soaked bandage on it and winced in pain. He had been placed in a hut near the river with sixteen other young Xhosa aged sixteen to nineteen years. They had for six weeks been disciplined, served a sparse diet, cleansed and lectured to. Their bodies were painted in black mud stripes and their faces had been painted with white stripes. All participants were made to run, to fight, to dance and to chant and grunt while so doing, in order to prepare for the event.

The ceremony was meant to mark the passage from boyhood to manhood. Only the fit and those of age and considered to be sufficiently worthy were invited to take part. Failure to be invited, or refusal to attend was tantamount to disqualification from their niche in the multi layered societal structure of their clan. Those who partook and passed were accorded the rights and privileges of young tribesmen. When the "abakweta" or ritual circumcision was performed on him with an instrument that was none too sharp, Sipho fainted. He had of course inhaled marijuana beforehand, as had the others, it being a common practice of the tribal inhabitants of the Transkei. Marijuana grew abundantly and the smoking of it had been reintroduced to him in the ritual circumcision training in the hut, which now had the pervasive odour of body sweat, blood and marijuana. The others, once circumcised, had run screaming or howling towards the river to the sound of drums and chanting by the elders. But he had fainted and had remained in the hut, thereby disgracing himself before his peers and before the elders

Slowly and in great pain, with the limited strength he could muster in his agonised state, Sipho dragged himself to a sitting position, turned over and crawled out of the hut, like a dog slinking into the night. He knew he could not remain. The hut was soon to be burned together the clothes, bandages and ritual items. The circumcised were now men He, however, had lost face. He would crawl away, hide, and if he made it through the night and the next day, he would make his way from his tribal village to Umtata, the nearest town and capital of the Transkei. He was not sure he could make it. Somehow, he did and from there he eventually came to Egoli, "The City of Gold" or Johannesburg, as it was called, and Sipho, the son of a minor chief of a minor tribe of the Amopondo branch of the Xhosa people, became in time the head of his country. Not in his own right, but through the machinations of the powers that be or perhaps the gods of his forefathers.

LIST OF MAIN CHARACTERS

SIPHO BANDISWA .... Later to become Belson Bandiba and awarded the Nobel Prize for Peace.

BELSON BANDIBA .... Freedom fighter, Lawyer, incarcerated for many years in Robben Island and in Pollsmoor Prison.

M.W.MOTHA .... Prime Minister of South Africa in the Apartheid Era.

WILLEM WASSON .... Physician, Head of Project Coast, a Division of The National Intelligence Agency of South Africa, Delta G Scientific and Roodeplats Research. He worked on numerous projects related to chemical and biological research.

LEONI MARAIS .... Researcher, Dept of Information of the National Intelligence Agency.

ANDILE MOTSWETSA .... Chef in the Kitchen, National Intelligence Agency.

PIETER BURGER .... Endocrinologist, Head of the Embryology and Fertilisation Research at Delta G Scientific.

EDWARD G FORRESTER .... Head of the Central Intelligence Agency of the United States of America.

DONALD R KEAGAN .... President of the United States of America.

MURIEL HATCHER.......................... Prime Minister of the United Kingdom.

ARCHBISHOP FRUTTOO .... Head of the Anglican Church of South Africa. Nobel Peace Prize Winner.

S. B. VAN BLERK .... Prime Minister of South Africa and Nobel Peace Prize Winner.

BINNIE BANDIBA .... Political Activist and wife of Belson Bandiba.

CAPT. HUGO RETIEF .... South African Security Police, Covert Operations.

PRINCE BAGISULU FATULESI ...... Chief of Zulu Nation.

The Transkei is an area of rolling hills and rivers in the Eastern Cape in South Africa. Here, amongst the verdant valleys and lush vegetation, live the tribes of Xhosas, Thembus, Pondos, Bhacas, Fingos and Maluti. The Malutis speak Sotho. The other tribes all speak Xhosa, a language characterised by clicks made by placing the tongue against the front of the hard palate and briefly drawing in air between tongue and palate. In the word Xhosa itself the "Xh" sound is a click made in this way. The Xhosa language is spoken by about twenty percent of the inhabitants of South Africa. The Xhosa tribes, as indeed most of the African tribes, have a complicated hierarchy of chieftainship and succession. Marriage to a member of a lower or "left tribe" can negate succession to kingship and chieftainship. One member of the tribe, a man called Badla Henry Bandiba suffered in this way. Due to a union between a woman of a "left tribe" and his great grandfather, the great grandfather (and his successors, including Badla Henry Bandiba) was forbidden succession in line to the King of the Xhosa people. Nevertheless Badla Henry Bandiba was accorded the rights of a minor chief.

In the village of Mveza in the district of Umtata in the Transkei in the Union of South Africa as it was then called, a son was born to Badla Henry Bandiba and one of his four wives. The son he called Belson Bandiba.

Badla Henry Bandiba was considered a troublemaker

by the ruling British colonial authorities and they deposed him of his rights to a stipend and other privileges usually given to minor chiefs. Badla and his family of four wives and many children moved to Qnu where they lived in relative comfort. This was due to the fact that Badla had sufficient cattle and wealth even without the stipend.

So here, amongst the green hills, some good farmlands and herds of cows, Belson was raised. He was a bright child, a good cattle herder and was by a combination of good fortune and intelligence, admitted to a mission school where he received an education not usually attainable by his Xhosa peers. Notwithstanding his education in the arts of reading, writing and arithmetic, all in English of course and given by priests and nuns, Belson, like his peers were first and foremost tribal sons and adhered to tribal practices. One of these was the ritual of circumcision at around the age of sixteen.

And so it was that Belson Bandiba joined Sipho in the hut where circumcisions took place. During the pre-circumcision training they had hardly said two words to each other. Belson was of a superior clan, related by birth to royalty, and even though his ancestors had been demoted from the hierarchy and the possibility of succession because of the bad marriage of Belson's great grandfather, Belson carried himself, indeed considered himself as better than Sipho. Perhaps he was. He did not faint. Sipho did.

Their paths were to cross again many years later.

CHAPTER 2

1983.

He was given a suit, a white shirt and a tie for the outing. Belson Bandiba is driven by car from Pollsmoor prison accompanied by three policemen. It is a bright morning early in April. It was in April two years before, on a similar crisp morning that he had been driven to Pollsmoor, the prison which was to be his new abode after so many years incarceration on Robben Island. He was now being taken by car to Cape Town. He had been told he was to meet with M.W. Motha, head of the government which had ordered his detention in Robben Island prison and then in Pollsmoor prison.

He knew that Motha, knick named "The Crocodile", was by reputation tough and unyielding. Bandiba considered Motha to be a wily politician and he knew that Motha was intelligent enough to know that anti South African opinion and sanctions against South Africa were hurting the country. There were increased rumblings of dissatisfaction from within Motha's own white political party. The disenfranchised black majority in the country was seething with discontent which could not be contained for much longer. Bandiba surmised correctly that Motha found himself beset by challenges and problems worsening day by day.

Bandiba, sitting in the back seat, between two white policemen asked himself "What does the Crocodile want from me now?"

The car was parked in the shade of some trees behind

the Houses of Parliament in Cape Town and quickly and quietly Belson Bandiba was ushered in via a back door into a small passage and then into a large room which was sumptuously furnished.

As he entered, M.W.Motha came in from a door at the opposite end and the two men walked towards each other, meeting halfway. They shook hands, politely said "Good mornings" and then with a wave of his hand M.W. motioned to Bandiba to sit in an armchair. Bandiba declined tea or coffee.

M.W. was a tall man. His baldness further emphasised his egg shaped head. He had piercing eyes, made larger by his spectacles, which gave him the look of an owl. Indeed, Bandiba thought he looked more like an owl than a crocodile. He was slightly stooped. He held his head forward much like a tortoise, as many tall stooped men are inclined to do. He wore a grey three piece suit, with a close fitting waistcoat. This appeared to be too tight for him and the buttons there seemed to be on the point of bursting. A chain from one of these buttons led to a pocket in the right front of his trousers, where a gold pocket watch was kept. He had a lighter grey handkerchief protruding from his left jacket pocket. The grey matched his complexion.

In contrast, Bandiba's suit was too big for him. As was his shirt collar size. This was because the size chosen was modelled on the suit and shirt he wore some two decades before, when he was checked in to prison to serve his long sentence. He was now nearly twenty years older. Prison and the passage of years had shrunk him. The prison warders did not seem to be concerned with sartorial elegance. Except for his greying hair and his aged face, Bandiba looked like a tall schoolboy in an ill fitting overlarge suit.

"I trust you are well," said M.W.

"As well as bird in a cage can be," replied Bandiba.

M.W. took in the reply without any noticeable outward reaction. His demeanour was that of a courteous gentleman, a far cry from the picture painted of him as an authoritarian, finger waving autocrat. M.W. removed his glasses. He wiped the lenses with the handkerchief which he took from his lapel pocket, and thought a while.

"Mr. Bandiba," M.W. said, "If the bird becomes a dove and when allowed to fly remains a dove, the bird can then be uncaged." The two men were alone in the vast room. They spoke for some twenty minutes. They then stood and shook hands. M.W accompanied Bandiba to the door through which he had come into the room. The policemen escorted Bandiba back to the car and he was returned to Pollsmoor prison.

Chapter 3

M. W. returned to his office in the Parliament building, picked up the telephone and said "Get me Dr. Wasson."

Willem Wasson, physician and cardiologist, head of Project Coast, a division of the National Intelligence Agency, Delta G Scientific and Roodeplat Research Laboratories was a smallish bearded man, in his late fifties. He was pleasant, with a sense of humor and dedicated to his work. This related to numerous projects. The funds allocated to his department were virtually unlimited. He was cognizant of similar work, "research", as it was called, by other covert agencies in the U.S.A., United Kingdom, China and the USSR.

Amongst projects he had researched was "How to Influence the State of Mind of Crowds." No successful drug or compound had been found as yet. Marijuana, ("Dagga") as it was called in South Africa, was used for centuries not only by many of the black population and but also by whites and "coloreds". Many rural as well as city dwellers were accustomed to its regular use. It was grown in many localities, some potent varieties coming from Natal and the Transkei. For controlling crowds it was not of much use. Singly, perhaps it could work. Drugs and compounds which would render black people infertile (or less fertile) were researched. Botulin toxins, nerve gasses (BZ), thallium, various organo- phosphates, cocaine, ecstasy, were all studied at Delta G and Roodeplat.

M.W. came to the point quickly after inquiring as to Wasson's health and that of his wife and children. "Willem, can you make a man who is aggressive and has set political opinions, become peaceable and docile in his views without his friends, colleagues, or even his spouse knowing?"

Dr. Wasson replied. "Sir, some tranquilizers are available which can influence aggression. They can have side effects such as drowsiness, have to be carefully monitored, dose controlled and administered, but will not necessarily change the persons mindset. Our knowledge of "happy drugs" such as ecstasy indicates variable effects, not necessarily, drug related but related also to external influences such as sound, light or even smell. No drug I know of can guarantee or produce change of political opinion and leave the person symptom free, unless it is very short term. Hypnosis, even mediated or influenced by drugs may work. There is no certainty. Likewise, subliminal suggestion. But again it is a question of trail and error. The Russians tried electro convulsive therapy on their dissidents, but they became rather like vegetables or lobotomized patients."

"Willem", said M.W. "We need to try. I mean you need to try. Or else we need a clone or a double."

CHAPTER 4

Dr. Willem Wasson paged through the report he had received from Professor Marius Pretorius who headed the Pharmacology section of the National Intelligence Agency.

He read the summary at the end of the report. Cannabis/Marijuana: Low doses can produce a state of well being or euphoria, a dreamy relaxation. There may be a more vivid sense of smell light and sound and changes of thought form and altered expression. The effects are believed to be mediated by the hippocampus of the limbic system of the brain, crucial for learning, memory, emotion and motivation. Stronger doses can produce shifting sensory images, rapidly fluctuating emotions, and an altered sense of identity, memory impairment, and dullness of attention despite an illusion of heightened insight, fantasies, hallucinations, image distortion and loss of identity. It may also produce a mellowing of mind in some subjects which is not necessarily dosage related. This effect is variable and may not be present in all individuals. The use of cannabis in many populations could be due to this effect which many users may find pleasing."

I know all this, he thought. Not too promising, but he had a plan which might work. In any event it was worth trying. He would attempt to modify a certain person's mindset. He knew the Prime Minister would authorise his plan.

Chapter 5

Belson Bandiba, by now the most famous political prisoner in the world, having been incarcerated for so many years, was not and would not be a dove. M.W. Motha had offered him his freedom in return for his assurance that he would renounce all violence (and in effect in Belson's mind give up the struggle against oppression and apartheid, which was the euphemistic name given to the policy by the regime.) This Belson absolutely refused to do. Giving up was not in his nature.

In his youth he had dreamed of being a boxer. Indeed he had gone to a gymnasium, had sparred and trained. The boxer in him was still there. Even in his imprisonment he would spar mentally, and spar and spar, until the time came for the knockout blow. Or his opponent threw in the towel.

Prior to his arrest, trial and incarceration, he had been abroad. He had left South Africa via clandestine routes to escape his oppressors more than once. He had travelled to several African countries sympathetic to his cause; he had been to England and to the Soviet Union. Wherever he went, he had solicited help, training, money, weapons and support for his cause.

He was now in prison. He had got used to his cage. He would not leave it unless by leaving he advanced his cause.

M.W. Motha knew this.

CHAPTER 6

Belson's sentence of life imprisonment for treason was considered harsh by most of the opponents of the white South African regime. Many others who were pro the white government felt he had been lucky not to get the death penalty.

His initial incarceration was in Robben Island, a small island a few miles off the coast of Cape Town, which had been transformed into a prison for political prisoners. Here the major work given the prisoners was toil in the stone quarries, a labour which was physically taxing and morally demeaning, especially to the intellectuals amongst the prisoners. The many hours in the hot sun, the inhalation of dust from the stones quarried and the back breaking work with pick and shovel took its toll on the health of the prisoners.

Belson was eventually transferred to Pollsmoor prison on the mainland. This may have been due to the authorities wishing to keep him away from the other prisoners in Robben Island who regarded him as their leader and mentor, or in response to mounting criticism from the outside world regarding his treatment.

Uprooted as Belson felt when he first arrived at Pollsmoor prison, his transfer had advantages. It was pure luxury compared to the Island.

Belson, of course pondered over why he and three other prisoners had been transferred from Robben Island to Pollsmoor. The conclusion he had come to was that in the world's eye Robben Island had become synonymous with the struggle against oppression and apartheid. To remove the leadership of the Black National Congress from Robben Island would perhaps diminish its iconic value as the symbol of the anti apartheid movement and perhaps also weaken the movement in the process.

He surmised also that some cadres in Pollsmoor prison were police informers planted there by the authorities. Many a time fellow prisoners would snitch to the authorities to obtain privileges or lighter sentences.

For certain, the quarters, the food, the lack of work expected from the prisoners, were all unexpected luxuries he found at Pollsmoor. It was, as his warders pointed out many a time, "a bloody holiday camp, for you sorry bastards" and that "they should thank their lucky stars." The food in particular, with some meat and vegetables, instead of the monotonous mealiepap served three times a day at Robben Island, was welcome.

Not only that, but soon after his meeting with M.W.Motha, a greater variety of dishes appeared. Some sweet, some savoury. All appreciated by the prisoners.

The warders were presented with the self same food as they had previously been given. Soon delicious cakes and cookies, previously freely served to the prisoners most meals, but not to the warders, began to be appropriated by the warders, especially when the senior warder was absent from the dining/serving area. This led to the "Cookie Strike". The prisoners went on a "Cookie Hunger Strike", refused their cookie less meals and the result was that the warders were given their own supply of cookies and not those of the prisoners.

Peace prevailed.

The improvement in the quality of meals was in no

small measure due to the arrival of a new cook at Pollsmoor soon after Belson's meeting with M.W. Motha.

His name was Andile Motswetsa.

He had started as a youngster in the kitchen of the Baviaanspoort Reformatory, gradually progressing to become assistant chopper upper at the Police Training College. Then Assistant Chef. He could read, had a knack for cooking, and was sent on a number of training courses, one at the Hotel School in Granger Bay.

Andile was a good listener, possessed of a good imagination which sometimes ran away with him and he was able to ingratiate himself with his superiors who were white policemen or warders, by reporting on the inmates of the prisons that he worked in. His career as a nark nearly came to an end when ground glass was found in his food, doubtless placed there by a disgruntled inmate who suspected him of being a snitch. He was violently ill, and after his "near death experience" as he liked to call it, he was transferred to the kitchen of the organisation called Delta G Scientific and Roodeplat Research Laboratories, both of which were part of the National Intelligence Agency.

Andile was given a change of name and put to work in the staff kitchen. He was quite a competent chef, hard working, even if inclined to partake of the bottle, which activity did not seem to affect his cooking ability. He progressed to Head Chef. The title was not one of admiration or awe, nor did it come with more money, but it made him very happy and indeed proud. It came with more responsibility for any kitchen problems that arose and he handled these quite well. Most of the staff, especially the senior staff, used the dining facilities as little as possible.

The senior staff was well paid and ate out as often as possible in fine restaurants, leaving the kitchen food for the lower staff echelons.

Andile was surprised one day when he was told to see Dr Willem Wasson, who he knew was very high up in the organisation, but with whom he had not previously had any communication. He was told to allocate his chef's duties to the other chef for the next few days and to report to a certain small office the next day to further his chef's training.

The next morning he found some cookbooks on the small desk in the office he was told to use. They were entitled "The High Art of Cannabis Cooking, "Marijuana Herbal Cookbook", "Grandpa's Marijuana Handbook" which was subtitled "Tried and Tested Recipes for the Over 50's"and also a video called "Cooking with Marijuana."

Andile was ordered to study the books and learn from the video. He was of course familiar with marijuana or dagga, as it was locally called. In fact in his informant days he had often told the police or warders about expected exchanges, dealers etc. He had reported prisoners' stashes. He smoked the stuff himself. He enjoyed it, partaking quite often.

That did not stop him from informing on others who smoked or possessed. He was by nature an informant. It gave him a sense of heightened importance and he had no qualms about reporting on others.

He paged through the books and sat down to study.

Chapter 7

Andile Motswetsa, having studied the cookbooks and the video tape, was told to try out the various recipes. He was transferred to Pollsmoor maximum security prison in Tokai and promoted to Head Chef.

The recipe books and video tape were taken away from him, but he was allowed to hand write and keep recipes he fancied. He was given a small salary increase.

Soon after his arrival the food and menu underwent change, not uncommon in the case of a new chef appointee. In particular the brownies, biscuits, small cakes and cookies proved to be popular.

There was approbation from the inmates and warders alike.

During the time of the new food program, officers of the National Intelligence Agency, in the guise of social workers, interviewed Belson Bandiba and other political prisoners for "routine detainee's prison checks". They had several talks with Belson. Two undercover agents engaged Belson in small talk and political talk during "exercise and fresh air outside time."

The social workers and undercover plants reported that Belson was still very much a hawk and not a dove.

After six months the new food program was slowly dropped. Andile Motswetsa was transferred back to his job as chef at the National Intelligence Agency. The handwritten copies he had made of the recipes he used were taken from him and shredded. The recipe books and video had already been taken from him. He was ordered never to speak of his time and efforts at Pollsmoor prison.

Chapter 8

Dr. Willem Wasson called to see Dr. Pieter Burger, Endocrinologist and Head of Embryology Research at Delta G Scientific.

He had walked to the laboratory and although he had scheduled an appointment, Dr. Burger was late as usual. Willem was not enamoured with being kept waiting. Nonetheless he waited in Pieter's office, paging through a dog eared magazine.

"Apologies, Willem", Pieter said as he appeared. "I was caught up in something". Wasson had never been to Pieter's laboratory when he was not caught up in something. Pleasantries were exchanged.

"Willem, are you here because of the negative report and lack of progress on my work in infertility?" asked Pieter. Pieter Burger was in his mid fifties, shortish, and had brown hair and thin gold framed glasses. He had on a white coat, looked like and was a scientist, a "boffin," well known in the fields of his expertise, namely embryology and fertility. Willem had indeed read the report. Most fertility researchers were engaged in treating the infertile "problems" of first world couples who could not conceive or procreate. Pieter was researching the opposite. How to decrease fertility in certain ethnic groups or populations.....en masse and surreptitiously. Willem had read the report and had been disappointed. In essence the report stated little of new import. There appeared to be no drug, no compound or medication, radioactive or otherwise, which would have selective effects and which when introduced into the food or drinking water of South Africa, would produce infertility in the black or "non white" population, but have no such effect on the white population. The report reiterated what he already knew. Contraception could only be achieved by the daily use of the "pill" or with the use of contraceptive implants or injections. These worked for three to six months, but could be made to work for longer, even perhaps for some years. Of course intrauterine devices, which worked for longer could similarly be used. All of these methods required cooperation from the subject, and most involved the use of medical or nursing or paramedical personnel and of course considerable expense to fund the manpower needed to implement.

The black or "non white" population would most certainly not willingly allow themselves to be subjected to such procedures. Contraception was a concept not popularly accepted by the black population. Indeed it was an anathema to them. Poor, hungry, and over populated as they were, they seemed to copulate like rabbits, often indiscriminately and with multiple partners, and procreate like rabbits, bringing many children into the world, most doomed to be poor, hungry and prone to disease and squalor.

Willem remembered a lecture he had attended in a black high school class, an educational contraceptive program, which attempted to show the class the merits of family planning. Slides were shown, one slide showing a car being driven by a black man with his wife and dozens of children all crowded into a medium sized car, looking squashed, hot and uncomfortable. The next slide showed the same man and wife in the same car, but this time with only two children in the car sitting comfortably in the back seat, all smiling.

"What does this tell you?" asked the teacher of one student in the class.

"It tells us that the man needs a bigger car," said the student. The class all agreed a bigger car was the answer.

The general mindset of the black ethnic group was that the more children the better. This, in spite of poverty, poor housing, overcrowding, malnutrition, and absentee fathers. Children were being reared by grandmothers, aunts and friends and not birth mothers due to breakdown or non existence of the conventional family unit and the need for many mothers to find work to sustain themselves at places far from their tribal abodes.

The small nuclear family concept favoured by the Western World (and harshly imposed by Communist China) had not made inroads in the "non white" population of South Africa. Despite three hundred years or so of contact with white culture and mores, the "non white" population still had their own tribal sexual ethnic cultural values ingrained. The more children the better. "No, Pieter. Tell me rather about cloning," said Willem.

"Not really my field, Willem," said Pieter. "It can be done in tadpoles and such like. Then there was "Dolly" the sheep in the UK." " No, Pieter, in humans, I mean," said Willem.

"Ag, man, these things are banned in most countries....but I guess it doesn't apply to us. Well, experimentally nothing yet has been a success. There were some Japanese researchers who claimed to have done it, or were they Romanian? Both of them probably hoaxes. There was a movie; I think it was called "The Boys from

Brazil," where some forty or so Hitler clones were supposedly made by Dr. Josef Mengele working in Chile or Argentina or somewhere after World War Two. It was a good movie. Still it was only a movie. Let us assume we could clone you, Willem. It would take many years for the clone to become an adult, that is, if it grew all right. Ag no, it is very problematic. The Italians seem to be into this type of work. I don't know what the Pope would say. I guess he would not be too happy. Maybe issue some edict or proclamation against it, I suppose. In theory, if one could modify or doctor a cell, say a person's stem cells in the bone marrow, one could maybe stimulate it to grow into an embryo or foetus …but this is far fetched and exists only in science fiction stories…."

"So nothing there, Pieter. I need an adult clone, chop, chop, now, not in fifty years time," said Willem.

"Sorry, man, nothing I know of Willem," said Pieter.

The meeting ended. The two men shook hands and Pieter Burger went back to his work.

He was researching an ingredient to be added to a popular beer, the locally brewed commercially made beer sold by the millions of cans and bottles and made by a large multinational brewery, which would produce infertility in the black men who drank it.

His work looked promising. He hoped Willem Wasson would not now take him off this project to work on producing a human clone.

CHAPTER 9.

Belson Bandiba had never had trouble sleeping. He often dreamt of his youth, roaming amongst the cattle he tended in his home village in the Transkei. He dreamt of his time in the mission school to which he had been sent. He enjoyed learning. While tending the cattle he recited the poems he had been taught in class. He said the "times table", he recited passages from the bible his teachers taught him. He dreamt of his time at Fort Hare College, his clashes with authority there, his role in the student society, where he held the post of chairman. He was good at his studies and eloquent of speech. He spoke slowly and his words carried an air of gravitas and conveyed sincere conviction.

He was expelled from his schools several times and later readmitted. After his expulsion from Fort Hare College he allowed to write his examinations in absentio, gaining a B.A. degree. His clashes with authority were always due to his insistence upon fairness and his struggle against discrimination. He dreamt of his past aspirations. He had wanted to study law, but was unable to obtain a position with any law firm to do his articles.

The law profession in South Africa was white. There were no black lawyers. There were a few Indian lawyers. These had obtained their degrees abroad and had been admitted, albeit reluctantly by the white dominated Bar Council.

He had approached several of them seeking a post to do his articles without success. Belson had applied to several white firms who turned him down. Eventually, however, he had, much to his surprise and delight, been offered a position to do his articles in the firm of Cohen, Glass and Goldberg. This was a small firm of Jewish lawyers. There was no Cohen and no Glass. These had passed away long before. There was Goldberg and a junior partner by name Fisher. He got on pretty well with his bosses. They did not mentor him, kept him away from white clients, but allowed him to attend "non white" or black clients. He remained with this firm the requisite time for articles, studied for and eventually passed the required examinations for law and for admission to the Bar. He was the first black lawyer admitted to the Bar in Johannesburg. Initially, the authorities were reluctant to admit him. They procrastinated and baulked at the very idea of admitting a black man as one of their own. However, they could find no statute or legal impediment, and eventually allowed him to practice law. The Bar Council tried to make use of his expulsion and clashes with the Fort Hare College officialdom in order to refuse him admission to legal practice, but as these offenses were not criminal in nature, the Bar Council relented. He was allowed to practice law.

One other black man, by name Bolivar Bambo, had been admitted to the bar by then. Belson Bandiba joined his practice. Bolivar Bambo was an older man. He and Belson became not only partners, but firm friends. Bolivar was already very involved in various groups engaged in the advancement of black rights. Belson was introduced to these groups.

It was Bolivar Bambo, who became Belson Bandiba's mentor in his legal practice, which truth to tell, did not do very well. This was because, not only was their clientele black and poor and unable to afford decent legal fees, but both Bolivar and Belson, raised the hackles of the white magistrates and judges before whom they had to appear to represent their clients, simply by being black and appearing before them. Still they did their best. They had no shortage of clients, only a shortage of clients who could adequately recompense them.

All the while, both men were active in the BNC (the Black National Congress) and various other groups and organizations promoting black enfranchisement and equal rights. The "Pass Laws", enacted by the government, whereby blacks could not live or work in the cities and towns, unless in possession of a "Pass" granting them permission to do so for a limited time, provided the practice with much work. Those who transgressed were placed on a train by the authorities and sent back to their tribal villages, if it was their first offence. Repeat offenders were liable to imprisonment. There were many such cases, and Bambo or Belson would appear requesting leniency. Other cases of theft, drunkenness, assault and the occasional rape provided the practice with much work. Pleading for leniency became the mainstay of their defense strategy for most of their clients. As the prisons were full to capacity, magistrates and judges were usually happy to impose lesser sentences in response to their "well reasoned" pleas on behalf of their hapless clients.

Belson Bandiba had by now become known to the authorities as a leading light in the Black National Congress. As was Bolivar Bambo.

Following upon the banning of the BNC by the South African Government, both men had gone underground, living secretly with friends and sympathizers, some black, some white, some Indian. They had to give up their legal practice. Belson was often on the brink of discovery and arrest himself, but managed to evade the authorities. The police had him on their most wanted list for not only had he become a leading light in the banned organization but he had been instrumental in obtaining weapons for the armed struggle, which he now advocated. The authorities were aware of his activities and things became too hot for Belson in South Africa. He was smuggled out of South Africa to neighboring Botswana, and from there he went abroad to several countries including Nigeria, Liberia, Libya and the United Kingdom.

He returned to South Africa several times, by underground means, to work with and to encourage his compatriots in South Africa. He was called the "Black Pimpernel."

Belson was eventually arrested and tried with others. The trail was a sensation, both in South Africa and world wide. It was known as "The Rivonia Trial" for it was at a farm called Rivonia where he and other stalwarts of the BNC and "Umkonto e Assega", the military wing, were arrested.

Chapter 10

Belson's accommodation in Pollsmoor prison was luxury compared to the Island, but it did not extend to radio or music. It was therefore with some surprise that a music system was one day brought and installed in his sleeping quarters. Some music was provided for him to play. Six CD's. Township jazz, some early New Orleans jazz, Count Basie, Duke Ellington, and Mozart.

No other prisoner had the benefit of this luxury. Belson discussed this with his fellow prisoners. He would tell his jailers to install music systems in all the prisoner's sleeping quarters or take his system out. Democracy was what he believed in. Democracy did not consist of extending greater privileges to one person. His fellow prisoners pondered the matter. They said that he should merely ask his jailers to provide music systems for all the other prisoners but in the event of the prison authorities not so doing he should not insist that it be removed. Belson asked his jailers to do so. He had from the beginning been given better accommodation than the other prisoners at Pollsmoor. When he asked his warders why he had been so singled out they said he should consider himself lucky. His fellow prisoners felt he should not make a fuss. Nothing was to be gained by complaining and Belson could lose his better quarters. But when the music was installed Belson asked that his compatriots also be given music. His request was ignored. In response to the question as to why he had music and the others had not he was then told "You are one lucky Kaffir to get music, especially as you are the worst of the lot." Belson protested about being called a Kaffir. The warder was transferred to other duties at Pollsmoor.

Belson had assumed, quite rightly, that as he was a high profile detainee, the outside world, if it got to know about conditions of his imprisonment, would be impressed that he was not being ill treated or treated as most black prisoners were as a rule treated in South Africa. News about, pictures of Belson (and his fellow prisoners) and the prison or Robben Island itself and of Pollsmoor were prohibited. By law, heavy sentences of fines and imprisonment could be imposed on the local press and media for any such transgression. But the authorities knew that the Red Cross, Humans Rights Organisations, the United Nations and others would insist on visiting Pollsmoor to see how he was being treated and some of these organisations would eventually be allowed to visit. South Africa's image was already that of the pole cat of the world and did not need further tarnishing. Perhaps the music would be seen as a positive factor by these organisations.

Belson's music system remained. It was left playing softly at night. Indeed he could not switch it off. It had been installed tightly affixed to the wall, high up near the ceiling. It was of what appeared to be unbreakable material, without visible wires. The music was preinstalled. Belson could choose whatever music he preferred from the six music selections provided by pressing one of six buttons. However, he could not turn the music off. It played continuously, morning, noon and night. The chosen CD, over and over, unless he got up to the installed music system and pressed the button to change the selection.

Belson once tried to silence the system by wrapping an item of clothing or towel around it, but the system's speakers were concealed in the ceiling's air vents and the sound came to his bedroom through the hundreds of small ceiling holes. He could not block these, unless he destroyed the entire ceiling or covered the whole ceiling. This would of course bring major repercussions.

He actually quite liked the music. He would have preferred a better and greater selection, but he was happy to listen to the music playing, even whilst reading or nodding off to sleep. The music played on and during his waking times and while he was asleep.

By coincidence, and Belson never gave it much thought, he had been examined by the prison doctor a week before the music system was put in place. The doctor seemed to pay a lot of attention to his hearing ability. He was a bit hearing impaired in one ear, the result of his boxing proclivity in his youth, but over all he heard pretty well. The doctor seemed happy.

Belson slept soundly. He always had. Perhaps the music system made him sleep more soundly. It did not change his political stance.

Subliminal audio mental modification programming, sometimes called sleep learning, did not work in his case.

This was reported to M.W.Motha.

CHAPTER 11

Belson had always been a sound sleeper. Several times he had slept through noise which would have woken most. On a few occasions he had nearly been caught by the police in his hideouts because he did not waken with the noise their arrival caused. He slept like a baby, and dreamed often. He could also "catnap" during the day. His head would drop, his eyes would close, he would commence to snore, and a few minute later he would wake up, refreshed. He did this if the company was boring, or during a movie or concert, especially in the dark. His "catnapping" caused him to get into trouble many a time at school. The snoring was a give a way and his teachers took offence. Once, in fact he had snored during a concert given in his honor in Amsterdam by Queen Juliana at the Rai Concert Hall while sitting next to her. This had caused him great embarrassment. But the Queen politely said she often wished she could sleep through many of the boring presentations she had to attend.

The music played in his room at Pollsmoor did not prevent his sleeping. It may have made him sleep even better, and during his repose he often dreamed.

He had one frequently recurring dream. It was the reliving of what was perhaps his finest moment. He was in the dock of the Pretoria Supreme Court of South Africa on 20th April 1964, delivering the opening statement of his defense case in the Rivonia Trial. The speech took four hours. The court, the reporters and the world at large, heard his words. He said forcefully and with em-

phasis "I am prepared to die". Belson repeated this statement three times. Portions of the speech he had made
came and went in his dream. He had opened with "I am
the First Accused."

Indeed, he was the first and foremost of the accused.
Those in the dock with him were also leaders of the black
revolutionary movement. Mostly they were blacks. There
were a few whites and some Indians as well. But Belson
stood out as the leader.

The accused were charged with training recruits in
the use of explosives for the purpose of guerilla warfare
for violent revolution and sabotage. In addition they were
charged with conspiring to act with foreign military units
when they invaded South Africa. It was also alleged that
they were promoting Communism and were soliciting
and receiving money from sympathizers abroad to fund
their aims and actions.

The prosecution stated that a six month supply of
munitions they were said to have was sufficient to blow
up a city the size of Johannesburg.

In his dreams Belson Bandiba relived parts of his
speech. He had said "In my youth in the Transkei I lis-
tened to the elders of my tribe telling stories of the old
days. Amongst the tales they related to me were those
of wars fought by our ancestors in defense of the father-
land. The names of Dingane and Bambatha, Hintsa and
Makana, Sgunthi and Dalasile, Moshoeshoe and Sekuk-
huni, were praised as the glory of the entire African nation"

"Some things so far told to the Court are true and
some are untrue. I do not, however deny that I planned
sabotage....We felt that without violence there would be

no way open to the African people to succeed in their struggle against the principle of white supremacy. All lawful modes of expressing opposition to this principle had been closed by legislation. We chose to defy the law. We first broke the law in a way which avoided any recourse to violence; when this form was legislated against, and then the Government resorted to a show of force to crush opposition to its policies, only then did we decide to answer violence with violence."

In his dream he saw the faces of the prosecutor, the judges, the defense team, the crowds of onlookers, the reporters and the court stenographers. His wife Binnie, his children, his supporters.

This dream occurred often.

Chapter 12

In other dreams Belson relived the time he had spent in prison in Robben Island, where he was incarcerated together with other "political prisoners" and several of the co- accused in the Rivonia Trial. He had been required to work in the quarries. Back breaking and taxing as the work was, it did not break his spirit. In Robben Island, Belson remained the leader and mentor of his fellow prisoners.

Depending on the weather, if Belson climbed to the top of the high mound of stones that had been quarried by the prisoners, a task which required good balancing skill as well as the presence of a disinterested prison guard, he could see Cape Town and Table Mountain in the distance. The years of his imprisonment on Robben Island prison had not been kind to him. Climbing to the crest of the quarry hill was not an easy task for Belson. But he climbed it as often as he was able. Sometimes he could see Cape Town in the distance, cradled by its surrounding mountains, At times through a haze of mist which gave the scene a mystical quality.

Many legends were told of the mountains, some believed to be factual, by the local population.

Van Hunks was a man who lived atop a mountain. He and the Devil had a smoking competition there. Van Hunks used an enormous pipe and won the competition. The Devil then revealed himself. Both he and the Devil disappeared in a puff of smoke. The puff of smoke became the cloud or "table cloth" which often still appeared above the flat top of Table Mountain. Van Hunk's mountain became known as Devil's Peak. Legend had it that Van Hunks often returned to this mountain. Many believed that he did so to do Devil's work. Smoke or clouds above the Peak portended such evil.

The table cloth of cloud which covered the flattened peak of Table Mountain was a good omen. The Devil had gone away. Belson thought that the view he saw from the Island was what Captain Jan Van Riebeeck, sent by the Dutch East India Company to Cape Town some three and a half centuries before, must have seen. His three small ships entered Table Bay. Van Riebeeck had been sent to establish a half way house or settlement to help sustain those on the ships plying the Spice Route from Europe to India .The mountains, now called Lions Head, Devils Peak, and Signal Hill, flanked Table Mountain, which was the "mother mountain," surrounded by her "child mountains." Van Riebeeck would have seen the mountains, the waves breaking on Blauwberg Strand, the green shrubs and the dark trees covering the slopes of the hills and mountains.

Jan van Riebeeck's arrival was the beginning of white immigration to South Africa. The clashes between white men and the indigenous San Bushmen and Hottentots and later with the black population were to come in the succeeding years. Who was there first? Probably the Hottentot population. The black races and the whites came to the Cape thereafter and probably at the same time. Clashes were inevitable.

What would have happened had there been a shorter sea passage or an easy overland route for spices all those centuries ago? Would there have been a Cape of Good Hope and a South Africa?

Robben Island was no more than twenty miles from Cape Town. Sometimes Belson's dreams were of his rescue from the Island. In these dreams he and his compatriots were rescued by an armed force of "Umkonto e Assega", the underground military wing of the banned Black National Congress. This never happened. It actually had been planned several times by "Umkonto e Assega" but never came to fruition.

He dreamed most nights. Those relating to his life of many years in prison were for the most bad dreams. He had two other dreams, set in the future, which came to him. In the first dream he was in a helicopter tied by ropes around him. The next sensation he had was of a blast of air and much noise as the helicopter door was opened, then of his body being bundled out. Belson felt as though he was suspended above the earth momentarily and then plunged downward. After that darkness. The dream always ended in darkness. This dream haunted him, even in his waking moments.

The other dream came to him only once or twice and it pleased him. He dreamt of a South Africa where democracy prevailed and all lived in harmony. This dream never came to fruition. Would that it had.

Belson had no control over which dreams the night would send him.

Chapter 13

Leoni Marais was a senior researcher in the Department of Information of the National Intelligence Agency. She was petite, had dark hair and a good figure, which she preferred not to emphasise and hid to some extent by wearing loose clothing. She wore dark rimmed spectacles which completed her school marm like look. Her attempt to play down her sexuality by her mode of dress and eye wear was not really successful. Women envied her. Most female co-workers felt she had achieved her high position in the National Intelligence Agency with her looks and not ability, while her male co-workers were happy to be at her beck and call and went out of their way to do her bidding. In fact she was pretty good at her job.

Her brief was to go over and further research the background and family of Belson Bandiba and to find a possible double.

She knew the following. Belson Bandiba was born in a small village in the district of Umtata in the Transkei. His father was a minor chief who seemed to have a stubborn streak and after a dispute with the local white magistrate, who was of course appointed by the colonial authorities, he suffered the loss of his stipend and his position as head man. He lost most of his herd of cattle and land. Still, compared to others in his village, his father was comfortably off. Belson was one of eleven children. He had four sisters. Belson's own history showed a similar stubborn streak as his father. His tribal name meant "from a wattle tree", but colloquially meant "trouble stirrer", and from his history of expulsion from school, his disregard of laws, his political views, his imprisonment, the name seemed to suit him.

He had a great deal of intelligence and at an early age was admitted to a Methodist mission school, where he learned the fundamentals of reading writing and arithmetic. Nevertheless outside of school, he remained a cattle herder looking after what was left of his father's herd. Tribal traditions, tribal obligations and tribal rituals were part of his daily life. He went to a Wesleyan run high school, and did well enough to be accepted into Fort Hare University in Alice, a small town near King Williamstown. Here he soon became engaged in student politics, student protests, and was arrested several times.

He and some fellow students protested against matters small and large. The protests were directed against authority, cafeteria food, examination time tables, white government restrictions on black education, black land ownership, and pro fundamental human rights. The list was endless. He revelled in protests, marches, speeches, student sit ins, examination walkouts and was most times the leader or instigator.

Leoni felt his nickname "trouble stirrer" was well deserved.

Belson came into contact with several leaders of the Black National Congress Youth Wing and was at one time head of the wing. He subsequently rose to high leadership of the Black Congress. When this organisation was banned he fled South Africa, went to the Soviet Union and to the United Kingdom. He returned by underground means to foment revolution against the white government in South Africa and headed "Umkonto e Asssega", the military wing of the Black Congress.

He was eventually arrested, tried, and sentenced to twenty years imprisonment in Robben Island for treason. Here he joined other luminaries of the Black Congress, also imprisoned for treasonable or anti government acts.

Leoni thought his imprisonment was well deserved. Publication of photographs of Belson Bandiba had been banned ever since his incarceration, so few knew what he looked like as he aged during his long imprisonment. This, thought Leoni, would make the search for a double easier. She knew, of course, that he had become one of the world's most famous political prisoners.

She continued her search, reporting to her superiors that her efforts would take time.

CHAPTER 14

1936.

Sipho, had, after fleeing the hut of ritual circumcision, slept in a ditch. Not much sleep came to him.
His penis felt on fire. The pain was unlike anything he
had experienced before. He had tried to walk but found
the pain in his groin too severe. Before the sun arose, he
crawled to the local stream and tried to bathe his injury
in the hope that this would lessen the pain. The water
did no such thing. The pain seared through his groin and
body and he fainted again.

When the heat of the sun on his face and the buzz-
ing and irritation of flies settling on his body woke him,
he crawled to the shade of a wattle tree. There he found
an aloe plant. He tore at it with his teeth and extracted
some juice from it which he applied to his penis wound.
It seemed to help ease the pain. He made a bandage of
leaves, wrapped his member in it as best he could and
crawled the several miles to Umtata. It took him 4 days.
He had had no food, except for some berries he found
and only some muddy water that he drank from a puddle
he found en route.

He arrived on the outskirts of Umtata before day-
break. Good fortune came upon him when the first hut
he saw had clothing hanging on a makeshift line and no
inhabitants to be seen. The clothing was not only his size
but of stylish design and quality. He outfitted himself
with his fortuitous find and hastened away, now walking,

albeit stooped like a hunchback, in order not to soil his newly purloined clothes by crawling.

He decided to put as much distance as he could between himself and the hut from which he stole the clothing. He eventually arrived in the main street of Umtata, where he was greeted by a comely girl aged around twenty years who took a liking to him or his attire. They spoke briefly, she offered him some food and drink, and directed him to an acquaintance who she said needed help to move some goods from one shed to another. Sipho was in no position to help. The pain from his wounded penis was still there though not as severe as before, but he, being glib of tongue and possessing an innate shrewdness, sensed she and her friend could be strung along and that he could befriend them and make use of them for his own ends while it suited him. And so he did. He regaled them with stories and tales which they found amusing, and the moving project was postponed. Although of different clans, Sipho and his new found friends got along well. He remained with them for some weeks and borrowed some of their clothing, saying his clothes needed cleaning. He did not wear his stolen outfit outdoors for fear of discovery.

Sipho took care of his mutilated penis and it gradually healed. However, in the region of his foreskin it healed with a large lumpy protuberance which, because of its size, shape, position and pebbly hardness was to make him a considerably desirable sexual partner to all women. Of course, Sipho was unaware of this at the time, but once healed, his new found female friend and he engaged in sex when they were alone, and he realized his new prowess when his misshapen extension proved the source of much orgasmic satisfaction to his partner. This was to stand him in good stead in his future.

He could not remain in Umtata. It was too close to his village and there was no work to be had there. Moreover, Sipho was afraid to be found by his village clansmen, who no doubt would know of his loss of face at the circumcision ritual.

It was his dream to go to Egoli to work in the gold mines as did thousands of men from the Transkei. But he was under age and looked it. He could not sign up for work in the mines at the local mine agent because of this and needed permission of his headman or chief to do so. For those who were of age no such permission was needed. Once they signed up for work underground in the gold mines for not less than nine months, the mine agent paid the third class rail fare to the Witwatersrand. Here, gold reefs had been discovered and Witwatersrand had become one of the world's biggest gold mining operations.

Sipho had got tired of his new friends. He became bored with the girl's too frequent sexual demands, and decided that he needed to leave Umtata. He would venture forth, try his new found greatness at sex with other partners and seek his fortune elsewhere. He had no difficulty of conscience when he stole the few pounds he found in the tin box which belonged to the girl. His need to leave Umtata was great.

Dressing in his worst looking clothes, which had been borrowed from his friends, he went to see the headman of the tribe of Balutis, who by reputation was not averse to taking bribes or presents in return for "favors". The journey took him two days. He walked there. As a herdsman in his village he had been used to walking and climbing hills and was relatively fit. He had gone soft in Umtata. The walk was a trial which he did not find easy.

Once there at the first village of the Balutis he asked to be allowed to see the headman. He was directed to the headman's kraal. In exchange for a handsome gift of tobacco the headman gave him a note stating that he granted Sipho permission to work in the gold mines. Sipho also extracted a promise that the headman would not tell his own village clansmen of his doings. This promise cost him more tobacco.

Sipho went to the office of the mine agent. He signed up for work in the mines and was given a third class ticket to Johannesburg or Egoli, as it was also called. Sipho said no farewells to his Umtata friends. He boarded the train.

CHAPTER 15

Sipho Bondiswa's journey to the Witwatersrand by train was a route which thousands of fellow Transkeians had taken. They travelled in the third class carriages, which were too few and which were always overcrowded. He had managed to secure a window seat. The window glass was stained and dirt encrusted and the window was only opened in part. Sipho strained and managed to open the window further. It was unpleasantly hot and stifling in the carriage. He needed more air. Sipho kneeled on the hard wooden bench seat and placed his upper torso, head and arms out of the window opening to see the view outside and get more air. The soot from the train's engine blew onto his face, and into his nose, but the sunglasses that he wore and which he had stolen from his Umtata friends, protected his eyes. The air from outside was fresher than that inside the compartment. He felt the contrast of the cooler air upon his face and the sting of the hot soot particles as they settled on his face. Soon his face became blacker in color than his complexion.

His fellow passengers, upon seeing his face, laughed uproariously when one wag remarked "How, man you are now so black you must travel in the fourth class compartment." Blacks were allowed to travel only in the third class carriages. Whites and coloreds travelled first or second class. There were no fourth class carriages. Sipho laughed along with his compatriots. He saw the humor in the remarks. He enjoyed the view and the air, and so he kept his head out of the window for long periods.

The first part of the journey, along the Wild Coast to Port St. Johns was indeed scenic. It was less so en route to Middelburg and then to Johannesburg. He became bored with the sight of endless shrubs and the barren landscape. Sipho drew himself back into the carriage. He tried to doze off to the clickety- clack of the train wheels upon the tracks.

In the Witwatersrand of South Africa, gold had been discovered. It was present in gold reefs underground. For the most part, deep underground. Mining for this precious commodity necessitated the construction and sinking of shafts many thousands of feet below the surface and boring and shoring up tunnels off the main shaft in order to hack away tons of the gold bearing reef ore. Then it was necessary to haul the ore up to the surface where it would be crushed and treated so that the gold could be extracted, refined and then sold to the world.

Gold had made South Africa what it was. It had brought in "Uitlanders," foreigners from Europe, England, and America. They were the engineers, entrepreneurs, financiers and workers ranging from electricians and carpenters to fitters and turners, many of whom had mined for coal and minerals abroad and men who had toiled and had experience of work deep within the bowels of the earth in tunnels elsewhere.

The majority of the workforce was recruited locally in Southern Africa and was black. They came from the towns and villages and rural plains of the Ciskei, from Pondoland, from Basutoland, from Zululand, and from the Transkei. Many of these territories, or "Bantustans" or "Homelands" such as Gazankulu, Venda, Bophuthatswana, Lebowa, Kwa Ndebele, QwaQwa, were poor in

soil or water and their inhabitants lacked farming expertise. Their populace, with the exception of their chiefs,
and apartheid government appointed ministers, were dirt
poor. The apartheid government had introduced a poll
tax on all adult black men to encourage them to seek
work. There was little work to be had in their homelands.
Pass laws prevented their migration from their homelands, but employment was to be had in the goldmines.
The men went to toil in the mines to be able to pay the
poll tax. And they earned money over and above the poll
tax which they took back with them or sent to their kin,
or spent in the bars and fleshpots of the townships which
housed them. Some miners came from far afield, from
Mozambique, from the Congo, from Zambia and even
from countries as far North as Nigeria.

On arrival at the mine compound, they were given
a perfunctory medical examination, issued with mine
clothing and a headlamp, and housed in male only
dormitories in the compound. Meals were provided. Ad-
equate, not sumptuous, much like prison fare, but more
nutritious. Kaffir beer was available, well liked and indeed nutritious. These men toiled long and hard deep in
the bowels of the earth, often crawling in and along tunnels which were small and too narrow to allow anything
but a crawling posture.

The more intelligent and industrious of these men,
once no longer rookies were elevated to the position of
"boss boy". They were then paid a little more and placed
in charge of a mine squad of "Boys." "Boy" was the generic term for these brave men upon whose sweat the
wealth of South Africa was founded. The white workers
in the mine were the overseers of the black workforce.

They had vastly better salaries, lived in individual homes, better built and styled than mine workers elsewhere in the world could attain. They were the engineers, the demolition or explosive experts, the carpenters, and the other many trades needed to serve and run the mining industrial giant corporations of South Africa. They were called "Baas", the word for boss by the "Boys." So the workforce, beneath and above the ground of the many gold mines in South Africa was divided into "Boys" and "Baasses."

When Sipho Bondiswa fled the hut of ritual circumcision his penis was bruised and hurting. So was his ego. However, signing on to join the brave men of the mine workforce to toil underground was balm for his bruised ego. He felt strong, a man, not a youth. He was now to become a gold miner. He looked forward to seeing Egoli, or Johannesburg, as it was also called. There he would make his fortune, or so he hoped.

Chapter 16

Sipho arrived in Johannesburg, tired, but happy and elated. He was one of thousands of recruits. His mere presence among them, gave him pride. Egoli was the City of Gold. It had appeared in his childhood fantasies. Tales of brave doings, manly pursuits, easy women, fortunes to be had, all in Egoli, had fueled his imagination.

He was soon to be disappointed. He did not find the streets paved with gold, as he had thought it would be. They were dusty and dirty. In fact only the main roads, where the white businesses were and the suburbs where the whites lived, were tarred or paved. The other roads and those of the townships around Johannesburg were dirt roads. No tarring, no paving whatsoever.

He trudged behind the many other mineworkers to the Diepkloof Mine to which he had been allocated. After a half day slog, the mine stood out before him. It comprised a vast area, all encompassed by high barbed wire, with the tall mine headgear and a huge yellowish white mine dumps as its salient features.

There were many buildings within the compound and security guards at the gate. Mine workers ending their shifts streamed out of the main shaft, their faces and work clothes smudged with a mixture of dust and sweat. Those workers about to start their shift lined up in two's and threes awaiting their turn to enter the cages which would propel them into the deeper parts of the mine. The lines were long. The shift workers numbered thousands.

There was much noise from the equipment and the hammer drills, clanging, banging, and whirring, orders being shouted. There was an all pervading acidic smell from the refining tanks. The African sun produced shafts of rays illuminating the dust particles in the air. There was singing and chanting from the miners as they entered the mine shaft cages to be lowered into the bowels of the earth to proceed to the tunnels.

They sang warrior songs repetitively, reminding Sipho of the chanting during his time in the ritual circumcision. His feelings of weakness and cowardice returned. The eagerness at becoming a mineworker vanished. Fear replaced it when he descended down the mineshaft at high speed in the small cage. The acrid smell of the dust of ground granite and dynamite was all pervasive. The tunnels were dark except where illuminated by bare small light bulbs. The miners had head lamps on their protective helmets to see by. There was heat and sweat, the noise of pneumatic drills, and a feeling of claustrophobia in the tunnels. This, Sipho thought, was what hell would be like.

The "Boss Boy" yelled and screamed at him. He could not use the pick and shovel as could the others. The "Boss Boy" called him a "Pretty Boy", slang for faggot. He yelled and taunted him. Sipho fainted. He was taken topside, looked over by the black mine first aid worker, given some water to drink and sent to the infirmary, to await the mine medic. He did not wait for the medic to appear in the infirmary first aid room. Sufficiently recovered, Sipho slipped off his bunk and slunk out of the infirmary at the first opportunity, before the medic arrived.

He determined to leave the mine. He rushed to his quarters in the mine compound. From there to the ablution block, where he showered in the communal shower. Dressed in his best clothes, he left via the main entrance gate. He took his small stash of money with him. Sipho told the guards at the gate that he had to go to visit his dying sick sister immediately.

He went up to the first taxi, one of many battered old cabs lined up outside the entrance at the taxi rank and asked to be taken to the nearest shebeen in the vicinity. Sipho tried to sound as though visiting shebeens by taxi was what he was accustomed to. His voice trembled, betraying his attempted bravado. He felt as though he was escaping from the confines of a prison. The cab driver sensed his nervousness and was happy to do his bidding. The driver also determined to overcharge him. He could see by the fine clothes on Sipho that he could afford it.

Shebeens were the illicit bars which sprang up wherever the black male population congregated and in the townships where they resided. Sipho had heard of shebeens from those men in his village who had been to Johannesburg and he was anxious to try one. He quenched his thirst and raised his spirits by drinking "kaffir" beer, a brew much loved by the black male population. Sipho liked it. He felt he could develop a taste for it. Some money remained from the bundle of notes he had purloined from his girl friend in Umtata. Sipho's youthful looks did not preclude his being served the beer. Shebeens were illegal operations. No laws regarding serving hours or age of patrons applied and for the most part the police turned a blind eye to the shebeens.

CHAPTER 17

Sipho's good looks, and his stylish outfit, the self same clothes he had stolen from the washing line outside the hut in the outskirts of Umtata, again stood him in good stead. The daughter of Mamma Thumba, the shebeen owner, served him his beer. They got to talking. He was invited to her home in Sophiatown Township. Mamma Thumba, big, fat and gregarious, and her daughter, called Beauty, were charmed by Sipho's outward appearance and his manner of talk. Mamma Thumba preferred that Beauty associate with Sipho rather than with the older men she met at the shebeen, who she knew had only one thing in mind regarding her daughter. Soon however, Sipho was doing the very same thing to her daughter, namely having sexual intercourse.

Beauty, by no means a novice in regard to sex, had discovered the joys of Sipho's penis. She had never come across a penis like this before and she was determined to make full use of it, often and whenever possible. However, she pretended to her mother that that her friendship with Sipho was platonic. Mamma Thumba, shrewd in business and in life, knew that Plato was not involved, but knowing Beauty's proclivities, she felt that Beauty's association with the young Sipho was somewhat better for her daughter than her sleeping around with all and sundry. Sipho moved in to Mamma Thumba's home. No more mine work for him.

Chapter 18

The years went by. Sipho married Beauty. They inherited the sheeben from Mamma Thumba when she passed away quite suddenly from a heart attack some five years after they had married. Sipho and Beauty had no children. Sipho thought that this was due to his misshapen penis. Beauty told him she did not need children. This was a rarity amongst black women. She had no maternal instinct. She had an instinct for making money and she and Sipho ran the sheebeen.

Their sheeben did well. Soon he and Beauty opened another, and then another. They prospered. But with the ownership of three shebeens, there were more demands for payment of "protection" money to various gangs. There was more "turn- a- blind- eye- money" needed to pay off the police as the shebeens were not legal and although usually left to operate, police raids and closings now and then did occur. Prevention, in the form of a bribe, was better than cure. The three shebeens were more up market than most and their clientele more elitist. They frequented the shebeens belonging to Sipho and Beauty in the knowledge that police harassment would be very unlikely. In fact, many of the elitist patrons were the high flyers, the movers and shakers of black society, the middle class, now growing steadily. Some were small business owners involved in various profitable enterprises, and some others successful in shady deals and crime of various types.

Still, there was more than enough money generated

by the businesses. In fact Sipho and Beauty were very well off financially. So they paid the necessary.

In addition to the shebeens, Sipho become involved in backing movie making. The fledgling local movie industry was growing by leaps and bounds. Movies with African content and local actors were being produced and gaining in popularity amongst local audiences. Sipho was the money bags. He was the producer. Sipho himself occasionally took small parts. He became a minor celebrity. There were newspaper articles and magazines about films and the film stars. A black Bollywood was being developed.

Leoni Marais, of the Department of Information in the National Intelligence Agency, spotted a photograph of Sipho in a magazine. She compared it with a recent photograph she had been given of Belson Bandiba. He looked, she thought, a lot like Belson Bandiba. She went to see one of the movies he acted in and she felt the resemblance uncommonly good. She obtained a recent video of Belson, surreptitiously made and she thought the resemblance uncanny. They way he walked and his body language were very much like that of Belson Bandiba.

Not only this, but his manner of speech sounded much like Belson. She arranged to meet with him in the guise of a reporter for the "Kaapse Rapport," a Cape Town newspaper. She had a thirty minute meeting with him which took place in his "office" in his main shebeen. She found him to be well mannered, soft spoken, charming and with a charisma she had not before sensed in a black man. He appeared self assured and when he offered her a drink, she accepted. He poured her a large single malt whisky of Scottish origin, in a fine crystal tumbler.

He seemed to be a man very much used to the best. He dressed stylishly. His office was tastefully furnished. Had she not been in a shebeen, she would have thought she was in an office of the chief executive of a successful business organization.

She agreed to go to a private screening preview of his latest film, in which he was playing the leading role. It was a love story, a soap, to be screened for television on a weekly basis in which he played a lovable but corrupt lothario.

The soap was to be screened for public television viewing the next month. Leoni reported her discovery of Sipho to the head of her department. She felt she had found a possible double for Belson Bandiba. The report went from the head of her department to the head of the National Intelligence Agency Covert Operations Department, Willem Wasson.

He studied the photos in the file he had before him, was immediately cognizant of the physical resemblance Sipho had to Belson Bandiba. He looked at the movies previously released in which Sipho had played minor roles and was further convinced. He looked at the tape of Sipho's forthcoming television soap, all copies of which the security police had confiscated from the distributors and from Sipho's office. Definitely a good resemblance.

Belson Bandiba had been imprisoned for many years now and circulation and publication of photographs of his likeness was forbidden. No one, except those who guarded him and very few others, knew exactly what he looked liked now.

Sipho could pass for Belson Bandiba. He had to be made to pose as and become Belson Bandiba.

First came the swoop by the Liquor Squad and the confiscation of Sipho's liquor. Then the Receiver of Revenue sent a dozen inspectors to what remained of his businesses and office and to his home. There was tax evasion a plenty. Possessions, expensive motor cars, television sets, jewelry, luxury goods aplenty, all unaccounted for in terms of where his income arose and which was undeclared. He received a hefty penalty for tax evasion.

Following upon his fine, he was arrested, and sentenced to fifteen years imprisonment, despite having good and high priced lawyers to defend him. He had been charged with crimes ranging from illicit liquor sales, running a disorderly house, fraud, illegal possession of firearms(which he had for his protection), possession and dealing in drugs(he did use himself and had dealt on minor scale). Living on the proceeds of prostitution was thrown in for good measure, even though it was common knowledge that in shebeens easily available women were the norm. By order of the court, publication of photographs of Sipho was not allowed. The case made headlines for a week. Most opined that Sipho must have offended someone high up in the police or government to be thus treated. Many other black entrepreneurs engaged in similar ventures were not so treated.

The case took one week in court. Its sensation lasted for around one week more and was then forgotten by most.

CHAPTER 19

Sipho become prisoner 33433430. He was issued with the drab prison uniform. His head was shaved and he was placed in solitary confinement in a small cell. He was not allowed out of his cell except twice weekly for a brief shower. No visitors were allowed. Neither his wife Beauty nor his legal representatives were granted access. It was as though he had disappeared. Disappearance of prisoners in the prison system was not unusual. It was accepted by the friends and relatives of the convicted as par for the course. Nothing could be done. If very lucky, sometimes the convicted person was released after many years of sentence. Chances of this happening were not good.

Sipho was placed on a diet sparse, but balanced, made for him by the prison nutritionist. His food was superior to that of the other prisoners. It was high in protein, but low in calories. This was meant to bring his weight down to that of Belson Bandiba`s. Sipho was deprived of reading material. He had no access to radio, television, or news of any kind. He was not allowed writing materials.

His life became a vacuum of desperate sameness. He had always been gregarious and fond of conversation. The daily routine of having nothing to do, no one to speak to, no physical comforts, began to take its toll. He had never been much of an intellectual nor had he read books or poetry.

There was little to occupy his mind. He could not remember nor recite any passages of those few books he had read in his school days. Sipho took to counting numbers or reciting the alphabet. He slept most of the time, becoming more and more depressed. He became dejected and began to contemplate suicide.

After five months of imprisonment, Sipho was taken to an interrogation room. Here he was seated, still handcuffed, to await the arrival of a member of the National Intelligence Agency who went by the name of Captain Hugo Retief.

Immediately upon entering the room, Retief ordered that Sipho's handcuffs be removed.

"Cigarette, Sipho?" he asked. Sipho had had no cigarettes since his imprisonment. He accepted gratefully. Capt. Retief lit Sipho's cigarette and one for himself, looking at the sign on the wall which read "No Smoking" and in Afrikaans "Nie Rook Nie". He shrugging his shoulders and waved dismissively at the sign, exhaling smoke slowly. "It's OK, man, we can smoke," he said. They smoked.

Everything OK?" asked Retief. Sipho, taking a long draw, shrugged and replied." Terrible, man."

"Ag no, sorry to hear this," said Retief. "Perhaps I can make it better. Tell me, anyone hurting you? ``

"No, Sir," said Sipho.

"They feeding you?"

"Foods OK. Nothing great. I've had better," said Sipho.

"But you were bloody rich, man" said Retief. "Here you are a prisoner, serving out your sentence, man. They tell me you are no longer rich. The state and those bloody lawyers of yours have taken it all away."

Sipho did not reply. What could he say? Retief was

in authority. To complain might bring worse upon him. Hard labor for instance. Or incarceration amongst hard core criminals, rapists and murderers.

Retief drew on his cigarette, exhaled slowly and said "They tell me you are a bit of an actor. Is that right?"

"I have acted in some movies," Sipho said.

"Is that so?" said Retief. "Were you any good?" Sipho did not reply.

"How would you like to act again?" said Retief. Sipho did not answer. He remained silent.

Retief said "You asleep, man?"

Sipho said "No, Sir. I don't know what you mean about acting."

"I mean play the best part any man could be offered. At the same time live a life of luxury. You will travel all over, first class, be respected, hell man, you would be like the Pope or Chris Barnard. Admired everywhere. You would have the world at your bloody feet," said Retief. Sipho said nothing. What Retief was saying seemed so far fetched that he thought Retief was either mad or drunk. Indeed, Sipho could smell liquor on Retief. His days and nights in the shebeen business had left him with a good nose for liquor on others.

"Think about it, man", said Retief. "I will see you tomorrow".

Sipho was handcuffed again and led back to his cell by the prison guard.

Capt. Retief did not come to see Sipho the following day. He waited until the day after. Sipho was once more brought to the small interrogation room in handcuffs. Again the cuffs were removed on Retief's order. Again they smoked. Retief came straight to the point. Sipho would be released from the prison he presently occupied, transferred to Victor Verster prison into a luxury cell, and then, once briefed over several months he would have to play the role of Belson Bandiba, the head of the Black African Congress, who was presently supposed to be serving out his sentence of twenty years imprisonment.

Sipho would be released as Belson Bandiba at the appropriate time. He would have to forget about his wife Beauty, his friends, his past life. He would to all intents and purposes be born anew.

Once released as Belson Bandiba, Sipho would do as he was told, speak as he was told, and lead if needs be the Black National Congress, which would be unbanned. He, as Belson Bandiba, would preach non violence, would advocate abandonment of all anti government and anti white policies, and reach an accommodation with the white government about power sharing.

In return, he, as Belson Bandiba, would live in luxury, have all the trappings of high political office, and would in a few years become the President of the new South Africa. Not only would his role as Belson Bandiba remove him from the twenty year incarceration he was presently serving, he would be serving his country, the blacks and whites alike, by making the transition to power sharing of government bloodless. A certain Evan Liko, a popular black activist had lately been killed by some whites. The country was on the eve of revolution. The government was doing this to prevent bloodshed. It was now willing to share power with the blacks, something never contemplated before.

The real Belson Bandiba, Sipho was told, was no longer alive. He had met with an unfortunate accident in prison. If word of his demise reached the public, riots, revolution and bloodshed was inevitable. The country would go down in flames.

Sipho at first thought Retief was mad. The plan was so far fetched. It bordered on the preposterous. But he questioned Retief and found that Retief had answers to all his questions. What about Binnie, the troublesome wife of Belson? She had not had contact with Belson for many years. But she would want to be his wife, wouldn't she, once he was released as Belson, asked Sipho. Not really, and only for face saving and to bolster her position as head of the Black Congress Youth Wing said Retief. Apart from Belson, she had had many lovers, and would be his wife in name only, said Retief. In due course, she would be dealt with. She was to be arrested, charged with various illegal acts, the foremost of which was a charge of being complicit in the murder of a teenage boy called "Shorty." Belson (Sipho) had nothing to fear from her. He would first separate from her and then divorce her. All would be arranged. Retief provided all the answers.

"What about my wife Beauty?" asked Sipho. "She will never be allowed to visit you, not as Sipho, nor as Belson," said Retief. "Later she will be told that you died in prison of "natural" causes."

Sipho knew about the deaths of prisoners from "natural" causes. He was afraid that if he did not accept Retief's offer he too would die of "natural" causes, as did many others in the prisons of the South African Police. They would surely not let him remain alive aware of the plan they had made regarding Belson's impersonation. Sipho considered his death in custody a strong possibility. Even if they let him remain alive, he would have nearly fifteen years of soul destroying incarceration ahead of him.

He remembered Belson Bandiba. He had no particular love for him. In fact he disliked him intensely. They came from the same valley in the Transkei. They were of similar ages. They were together in the same ritual circumcision hut from which Sipho had fled. They were distantly related, but Belson had been aloof and haughty towards him had looked down upon Sipho because Belson came from a "higher" tribe. Sipho had no claim to such lineage. It was irony indeed that Sipho was now being asked to be Belson.

He took up Retief's offer. He agreed to become Belson Bandiba.

CHAPTER 20

Sipho was transferred to Victor Verster prison in Paarl. Here he underwent extensive learning for his new part, that of Belson Bandiba. He was taught to emulate Belson's mannerisms and was given voice and speech lessons. He was taught the names, dates and history of incidents in Belson's life, and of events in the lives of his family, his "comrades" and his lawyers. Sipho was shown photographs of these numerous people and he learnt how to identify them. Particular attention was paid to important events in his life and the effect and ramifications they had on his life.

The study of Belson Bandiba's life was time consuming and as all encompassing as possible. It took months of hard work. He had the finest teachers and aids provided for him. It was an acting role the like of which he had not imagined he would have or master. Every two months he was tested on his ability to master his studied role. He was made to remember the important passages of his speeches, the names of his teachers, professors, advisers, children and birthday dates.

He had never been much into politics. He had achieved a comfortable existence and status in his past, working within the system of life and politics in South Africa. He had within him the distrust of all blacks regarding whites and the underlying concomitant loathing of the system and the white supremacy. But he was not versed in political theory or the machinations of the apartheid philosophy locally and its ramifications on the world stage. He was therefore tutored in this regard. The nuances were hard to learn and understand, but they amounted to this. South Africa for the black inhabitants. Whites tolerated only if agreeable to this, or if needed to contribute or play a role in the general welfare of the advancement of blacks. Overseas whites support to be encouraged and sought in order to achieve black objectives. The new Belson Bandiba, however, while maintaining this philosophy which he and his cohorts had crafted over many years to be still in place, would upon being released into the world, ensure that the whites obtained a fair deal.

It was not all work and no play. Every now and then he was given holidays to places such as luxury private game reserves with paid female companions. Gourmet food and drink was here provided, in unlimited quantities. He had been used to good food and drink in his previous life, but not of this quality. In Victor Verster prison, where he was studying his role, his food was only marginally better than routine prison fare. He began to look forward to the vacation rewards which were given him every two or three months. Here he could indulge his every hedonistic wish. Sex, food and comfortable surroundings. Silk sheets and silken lingerie.

He was delivered to these five star venues accompanied by members of the National Security Agency Covert Operation Squad who monitored his every move and picked up the tab. He was particularly vexed by the CCTV cameras which were installed in his bedrooms. His every move, including his sexual activities, was watched by his minders. The minders looked forward to these intimate moments. They were amazed and impressed by the cries of satisfaction of his sex partners. Sipho was not at first aware of the presence of the video cameras. He was very upset when he discovered their presence. His request for their removal was met by the response that if the videos went, he would be back in Victor Verster prison. Sipho decided not to give up the few days he had of living it up every now and then by insisting on the removal of the video monitors. In fact, knowledge that his sexual activities with the ladies were being watched inspired the actor in him. He was determined to give them a good show. In any case he was also monitored twenty four seven in Victor Verster. His minders knew when he urinated or defecated. When he brushed his teeth. When he masturbated. Let them see how he was enjoying his luxury reward vacations too.

There was some discussion among minders as to whether the misshapen protuberance on his penis should be removed, for Belson Bandiba did not have this, nor was Belson in his prime by any manner or means a "stud" of this magnitude. It was decided to leave his penis for the time being, so as not to upset Sipho. The most sympathetic of his minders and the most voyeuristic of them said "Ag man, let him enjoy his fucking. We fucking well need him."

Chapter 21

1979

Dr. Willem Wasson, head of Project Coast and various other divisions of the National Intelligence Agency of South Africa had also been Head of Covert Operations of the South African Intelligence Agency for some years. He had cordial relations with the Central Intelligence Agency of the United States.

Both agencies had mutual interests in countering the perceived Communist threat to the West. Both countries were inclined to see "a red underneath every bed." They cooperated also in the clandestine development and delivery of arms and military equipment even during the long period when such activities in relation to South Africa were embargoed in terms of United Nations resolutions. South Africa was considered a good friend and supporter of the West and the only reliable anti Communist bastion in the African continent. Cooperation extended to medical research as well. And so it was that the findings and discovery of a new deadly virus by a team of doctors, led by a Dr. Andre Pistorius, who was a researcher in the biomedical division of the South African Intelligence Agency, were handed to the Central Intelligence Agency.

Dr. Andre Pistorious had come across a number of strange illnesses which seemed to be associated with a decrease in immune response in those affected. The illnesses were of various types. He and his team were able to isolate a virus in most of the afflicted patients. They called it the Monkey- Chimp Virus 7, or MCV 7. They postulated that it came from monkey meat, which the chimpanzees had eaten. The meat of the chimpanzees was subsequently eaten as "bush meat" by members of local tribes. Some of these "bush meat" eaters later presented with various diseases. The virus seemed to have no visible effect on the monkeys or the chimpanzees. It appeared to have mutated to a form, which, if transmitted to humans resulted in decreased immunity. Some of these humans had very low white cell lymphocyte counts. Those infected manifested with various diseases, and often became emaciated and eventually died from lung disease or cancers.

Those with disease and low lymphocyte counts often had high numbers of the virus in their body secretions and particularly in their semen. It was postulated that the disease could be sexually transmitted.

Willem Wasson sent the virus specimens and the initial findings to the Centre for Disease Control in Atlanta in the United States of America. After some initial work to confirm the postulates of the South African researchers, the virus specimens and the research findings were sent to the Central Intelligence Agency Biological Research Division.

A similar virus was found in homosexual men in the San Francisco region. Virologists in the United States and in France believed they had isolated the virus. This became known as the AIDS virus, AIDS being the acronym for Acquired Immune Deficiency Syndrome.

The virus was also called the HIV virus, as it was associated with human immune deficiency.

The virus and the associated diseases had also been found in Haiti. The CIA research team felt the virus had a predilection for male homosexuals and for black people.

CHAPTER 22
1993.

Edward G Forester, head of the CIA drove alone, without his customary body guards, in a Ford Cortina which had seen better days. Asking only for an "unmarked car" from the car pool had served him right. To get a better car he should have specified a "decent unmarked car". The bodywork of the car he was given looked so old and in such poor condition that it would invite attention when he drove up to the Oakville Hotel in Arlington, Washington, DC, and handed it to the care of the parking valet. The hotel was four stars. The car would stand out as a sore thumb. Not even trades people, delivery persons and such like, who came to this hotel would be in such a jalopy.

Anyway, he could not now go back and get a better car. He did not want to keep the President of the United States of America waiting.

He recalled a secret meeting he had attended in the United Kingdom some years back. It took place at Bletchley Park and was attended by Muriel Hatcher, at that time Prime Minister of England, Donald R Keagan, President of the United States of America, M.W.Motha, Prime Minister of South Africa and himself, as head of the Central Intelligence Agency of the United States of America.

M.W. Motha thought he was invited to this meeting as South Africa was considered a bastion against Communism. He was in fact invited because of Dr Andre

Pistorious' work on the AIDS virus. But in fact Communism was not discussed, nor was the AIDS virus. The meeting decided no action plan.

No other persons were present. No notes were taken. No recordings made. Each participant had been given two documents marked "Top Secret/Not to be Copied/Destroy after Reading."

The first document was headed "POPULATION EXPLOSION---DOCUMENT ONE".

It set out in detail the predictions of exponential population increase and the dire consequences for the world and Africa in particular due to population increase.

Forrester said "Prime Ministers, Mr. President......if I may...please read the second document."

This document was headed "GENOCIDES AND POLITICIDE--DOCUMENT TWO

It too had been compiled by the CIA. In regard to the continent of Africa the following was noted in regard to loss of life due to politicides and genocide:

Country	Dates	Civilian Death Toll	Major Killers
BURUNDI	1959-1979	250,000 Hutus	Tutsis
		50,000 Tutsis	Hutus
SUDAN	1956-1979	2 million Nuer	Khartoum Govt
		Dinka	NIF
		Christians	Militia

		Nuba	Rebels
DEMOCRATIC REPUBLIC OF CONGO	1950-1979	200,000	Colonial Forces Rebels Army Kabula Rwandans
UGANDA	1972-1979	350,000 Lango Karamaja Acholi 100,000 Buganda	Amin Police/ Army Obote/ Police
NIGERIA	1996-1979	3 million Ibos Yarala Hausa Ogano Tvo	Nigerian Army/ Police

After silently pondering the documents for some time, Donald R.Keagan, President of the United States of America asked "So, what do we do?"

There was silence from the group. Then Muriel Hatcher, Prime Minister of England said slowly and with emphasis "Nothing, we do nothing, precisely nothing."

Forrester, head of the CIA cleared his throat and said

"Exactly, Document Two may well cancel out Document One."

"Precisely, precisely so", said Hatcher, "I saw that."

Forrester, scratched his head, stroked his chin thoughtfully, and said 'It may not be enough." He thought it politic not to raise the discovery of the AIDS virus and the research on it by the CIA. Better he should speak with the President of the United States before raising the issue.

M.W.Motha felt honoured to be invited to attend the meeting. He said nothing beyond a "good to see you" when he shook hands with the others attending the meeting. He left without anything of import being said to him, or without contributing anything of import himself. He flew back to Pretoria somewhat perplexed. Was he, and indeed South Africa, being allowed to come in out of the cold?

Chapter 23

Forrester continued his drive. He passed by Arlington Cemetery, the resting place of so many brave Americans who had sacrificed for their country, deep in thought and he became more depressed. He felt for the brave men and women who had died, and it felt strange that he was now going to see the President of the most powerful country in the world, Donald R Keagan, to propose death to so many more. Not soldiers, but humans nevertheless.

In a sumptuous suite in the Oakville Hotel, Donald R. Keagan, was putting into a sideways turned cup. The carpet was thick and very much like a golf course green and he was putting well. He felt his golf was improving. He wished he was on the golf course green.

A knock on the door and Edward G Forester entered. The two men were alone. No Presidential aides, no guards, no advisors. They exchanged customary greetings and the President enquired after Forester's family. They sat on two overstuffed armchairs, facing each other and spoke seriously for thirty minutes. Then the President said"OK, go ahead. Of course I never spoke to you in this regard. You never spoke to me. This meeting did not occur. Make sure it is not diarized or recorded."

"Yes, Mr. President, understood, Mr. President", said Forester. "Good day Mr. President".

They shook hands and Forrester left the suite. His mind was working overtime. What was he, with the Presidents consent about to do? Would he go down in history as an Idi Amin, or a Hitler, someone who proposes the destruction and extinction of a section of the human race?

Still, all things considered, sacrificing or better put, getting rid of some of the human population in order to save the rest of mankind.....perhaps that would be how he would be remembered if his activities or proposal succeeded and his actions came to light.

Chapter 24

In the meeting between Forrester and the President "that never happened" two issues had been discussed. These matters had been raised before at Bletchley Park some years prior. The first was that the rate of population explosion predicted there was under estimated. It was now postulated to become an avalanche. This was going to cause and was already causing massive depletion of the earth's available resources of food, energy and water, far greater than the earth's ability to replenish its resources. Carbon gasses, the greenhouse effect, global warming and toxic waste would increase by vast amounts. The result of all this, caused by and together with population increase would be a world of overpopulated, starving masses. What had been discussed and predicted at Bletchley Park three years back under "DOCUMENT ONE "had been a gross underestimate.

The second matter. Forrester had reported to the President the discovery of a virus which would, it was thought, selectively decrease the world's overpopulation. This virus had been detected in monkeys and chimpanzees in Central Africa by the researchers working for covert departments of the South African Intelligence Agency. They were researching methods of population control and population decrease. They sent the virus to the Centre for Disease Control in Atlanta. From there the CIA took over. The Centre confirmed the findings of the National Intelligence Agency of South Africa. The virus could be sexually transmitted. It had a predilection for the black population. It also appeared that male homosexuals, black or white, were very susceptible. The researchers felt that was there little likelihood of a vaccine or cure being developed due to the inherent ability of the virus to keep changing in form. The CIA biomedical researchers discovered the virus in the black population of some people in Haiti. They found it also in male homosexuals, black and white, in San Francisco. It was postulated that an airline flight attendant who flew to Haiti and later died of the disease was the source of the viral transmission to other homosexuals in San Francisco.

The President had given the go ahead to implement the viral solution to overpopulation

In addition during his meeting with the President, Edward G Forester had emphasized and the President had readily agreed that there was to be no "Tuskegee" story leak repetition in regard to this new deadly disease.

The infamous Tuskegee experiment took place from 1932 to 1972 in Alabama. In this experiment the effect of Syphilis was studied upon unsuspecting mostly poor and illiterate African-Americans. Penicillin, which was in use from 1947 and which could have cured them was withheld. The subjects in the study suffered the effects of Syphilis to which they had been deliberately exposed. When the media discovered this all hell broke loose and the presence of racism its ugliest form in the United States of America became a proven given. This, despite the repeal of racist laws and the "official" abandonment of racial segregation by the government of the United States of America.

Forrester carried no documentation with him, no notes or information relating to the virus. The scientists researching the virus both in the CIA and South Africa were cleared at the highest level and sworn to secrecy.

The plan regarding the Aids virus proposed and agreed by the President was not aimed specifically at African-Americans. It was aimed primarily at black populations in poorer countries world wide. These countries were euphemistically often called "Developing Countries." What they seemed to develop most was poverty, disease and burgeoning, starving populations.

The plan was to reduce their population numbers.

As a start the virus would be given to the black populations in African countries. The Covert Operations Division of the South African National Intelligence Agency would assist in the clandestine introduction and distribution of the virus. It could easily be placed in blood needed for transfusion purposes and given to black mine workers. In apartheid South Africa, blood collected from black donors was not given to white recipients. This was part of the apartheid philosophy. Blood was kept separate, for transfusion purposes anyway. There was black blood. There was white blood. Since the time of Van Riebeeck, some three hundred years back, however, there had been miscegenation across the color line. In more recent times, the apartheid laws made intercourse between blacks and whites and coloreds and blacks illegal. Despite this legislation, it occurred. Pretty frequently. The lineage of many a white often showed the presence of black or colored blood. But this was not made common knowledge. Most times it was well hidden. M.W. Motha himself was rumored to have colored blood in his forbears. But blood for transfusion purposes was kept separate, never mixed, in true apartheid fashion.

The black mine workers came from their homelands and from elsewhere in Africa, to work in the mines in Johannesburg in the Witwatersrand and in the Orange Free State Province of South Africa. When they needed blood transfused the viral contaminated black blood would be given them. They then went back to their homelands or countries of origin in the rest of the African continent. It was postulated that those infected would take the virus with them and transmit the infection. Also, of course, while away from their spouses who were left in their homeland villages far away, many of them were known to frequent black prostitutes. It was thought that the infection would be transmitted to the prostitutes, who in turn would pass it on to their customers, mostly other blacks. And so on. The contaminated blood given for transfusion for medical reasons to a small number of subjects would, by these "natural means" spread to many. The plan was simple. The implementation thereof was not going to be costly. It seemed, on the face of it, to be a good plan for reducing the black population.

In the United States of America, where the virus had been detected in male homosexuals, it was felt that the spread would occur there "naturally" due to the known promiscuity of male homosexuals, black or white. No iatrogenic method was needed. Other means for the transmission to the black population could be considered and implemented but would be held in abeyance in the meantime, pending the follow up study of the spread and epidemiology of the disease.

This was the plan for which Edward G Forrester had obtained approval from the President of the Unites States of America.

Chapter 25

M. W. Motha sat in the green leather armchair in his office. He opened the sealed envelope, marked "From the United States of America, Central Intelligence Agency, for the Eyes of Prime Minister M.W.Motha Only, Destroy After Reading." He took a sip of Rooibos tea, from the Royal Dalton teacup. When he had met the Queen of England some while ago, he saw that she too used Royal Dalton cups and saucers. Rooibos tea, or "red bush" tea, was said to improve mental facilities, digestive problems, and promote regularity. It was grown in his beloved Cedarberg. He loved Rooibos but Her Majesty preferred Earl Grey. So did Muriel Hatcher. He ran his hand over his bald head. He often did this when anxious or concentrating. He opened the sealed envelope, removed the plastic document holder that was inside the envelope and immediately entered the pin code he had been given to allow him to open the document holder without the contents self destructing.

The single page document was a report marked TOP SECRET from EDWARD G FORRESTER. It was an assessment of the work done by the Biologic Division and Centre for Disease Control in Atlanta. It also contained a suggestion for a possible method of population control. It was postulated that the black population and the homosexual population, could be controlled and even reduced by this method.

M.W.Motha studied the report. He took a sip of Rooibos, removed his spectacles and again ran his hand over his bald head. He felt happy to try to implement the method in South Africa and the African Continent.

The plan was slow in its implementation. After transmission of the virus to the subject, it often took years to manifest as the disease. Sometimes after transmission, no symptoms were evident. In those infected, where the disease symptoms developed, it proved to be the cause of great suffering and misery. It caused slow painful deaths in those who were susceptible. The disease did not confine itself to the black population and homosexuals, although it did have a predilection for these two groups. It caused death, but death came slowly. It did not work as had been hoped. The CIA and the South African Intelligence Agency denied their part in the discovery and propagation and evolution and spread of AIDS.

It was not effective as a means of black population reduction. However, it did infect hundreds of thousands. It was burdensome to the state medical facilities and nearly bankrupted the government hospitals. It produced thousands of orphan children whose parents had succumbed to AIDS. It infected newborn children born to infected mothers. It infected thousands of the work force, who died agonizing deaths. The President of South Africa, who succeeded Belson Bandiba, one Baba Bebeki, also a leading light in the BNC, did not believe that AIDS had a viral cause. He delayed the introduction of generic medication and retrovirals which could be palliative. His Minister of Health, a black lady doctor by profession, by name Manto Mabalala-Bbingo, who had trained in Moscow and Tanzania, felt similarly. She became the laughing stock of AIDS experts world wide and was called Dr. Beetroot, or Dr. Lemon, or Dr. Garlic when she advocated beetroot, lemons, garlic, and similar home remedies to prevent the disease and to improve health. Notwithstanding and despite this, AIDS did not reduce the black population significantly. The black population continue to burgeon.

Ironically, the disease struck several members of the upper hierarchy of the Black National Congress. Several of them eventually died of AIDS. It also resulted in the death of one Bakgat Bandiba, who was the elder son of Belson Bandiba.

Chapter 26

The education and training of Sipho proceeded. It appeared Sipho had a receptive mind and a willingness to learn his new role. He played it from the moment he woke. His tutors were mightily pleased with him. M.W. Motha, who was regularly updated as to his progress, decided that the time had come to free Sipho and release the new Belson Bandiba. Sipho had been briefed to become a dove. He would be set free. There would be a great media circus and the new Belson Bandiba would propose peaceful power sharing with the whites. He would reign in the militant hotheads of the Black African Congress. There would be elections in South Africa, and the black population would for the first time be allowed to vote. Notwithstanding the result of the poll, the whites would be given at least a fifty percent share in government. Apartheid would be abandoned. All discriminatory racial practices would cease. Racially discriminatory laws would be repealed. The "Immorality Act", which made sexual relations between whites and "non whites", in and out of marriage punishable by law, would be scrapped.

There would be forgiveness of all acts of aggression and violence, including murder committed by both sides during the apartheid days. Belson would use his position as leader of the Black National Congress to ensure all this.

If necessary a "Truth and Reconciliation Commission" would be set up.

There would be "free and fair" elections in South Africa. Notwithstanding the outcome of these elections, the leader of the "white" political parties would share executive power with the leaders of the "black" political parties.

The new Belson Bandiba would become the President of a new democratic South Africa. However the Prime Minister would be white and drawn from the "white" political parties.

It was a grandiose plan, one which depended on the Sipho, the new Belson Bandiba, now turned from "hawk" to "dove".

It was a complex plan, largely conceived in the mind of M.W. Motha. It was as far fetched as it was devious. M.W knew that failure of the plan would precipitate a bloodbath. But he knew also without this plan the Black African Congress and its military wing would sooner than later and probably very soon embark upon open warfare. The continued disenfranchisement of the black masses would cause the collapse of South Africa as he knew it.

M.W. Motha knew he had little time. There was dissention within his own political party. There was increasing political and economic pressure upon South Africa from the world at large for the release of Belson Bandiba, now imprisoned for twenty seven years and more calls for the rapid enfranchisement of the black population of South Africa.

CHAPTER 27

1989.

Sipho's education proceeded at an increased pace. Dissention within the leadership and rank and file of the National Conservative Party resulted in increasing calls for the stepping down of M.W.Motha. He resigned. He was replaced as the party's head by S.B.Van Blerk, a long time party stalwart. Van Blerk became the new Prime Minister of South Africa. He knew nothing of M.W's plan for the substitution of Belson Bandiba, the recalcitrant hard core leader of the Black African Congress, by the new amenable Belson. The project had been kept very secret even within the highest echelons of government. High ups in law enforcement and intelligence agencies were unaware of the switch.

M.W had to inform Van Blerk of the proposed switch. Van Blerk was initially stunned by the revelation. "Man, you could have knocked me down with a feather," he said when he spoke to Dr. Willem Wasson, one of the few men who knew of the switch and who confirmed the proposed replacement of Bandiba by the actor Sipho. Wasson was firmly of the opinion that the new Belson Bandiba was ready for release from prison. His tuition was as complete as it could be. Now was the time to place Belson Bandiba on the world stage.

Van Blerk visited Sipho in prison. He looked like, spoke like, and acted like Belson Bandiba.

Van Blerk was reminded of Shakespeare's "All the world's a stage, and all the men and women merely players. They have their exits and their entrances. And one man in his time plays many parts." He was convinced that a double had been created. It was time. The old Belson Bandiba would exit. The new Belson Bandiba would enter. Centre Stage.

M.W., "the Big Crocodile," had exited. The new Van Blerk had entered. He too would occupy Centre Stage.

South Africa could wait no longer. Revolution was in the air. Van Blerk revelled in the thought that he would be given the credit for peacemaking.

CHAPTER 28
1990

Prime Minister Van Blerk visited Sipho in Victor Verster prison for the second time. Van Blerk informed him that the moment had come for his release. The time had come for him to face the world. Once released, this would be his daily timetable. He would as per usual wake up or be woken up at 5.00am. He would be brought his weak tea and get dressed. His clothes would be ready laid out for him. He would, each and every day be briefed at 5.30 am. He would breakfast at 6.00 am or as soon as the briefing ended. He would then carry out his schedule. If at any time he was unsure of what to say or do, he was to ask to use the bathroom, or to have a short rest break. Once alone he would be able to communicate with his instructors by means of a tiny high tech transmitter placed within the hearing aid he wore in his left ear. At all times this same device was a means whereby he could be given immediate orders as to what to say or do in any situation that warranted such instruction.

His final test, before release, would be a meeting with his wife Binnie Bandiba, who had not seen him for over five years. She had written to the real Belson while he was in Pollsmoor Prison every few months. Sipho had read these letters. She had been told that he was not permitted to reply. She had spoken to Sipho, the new Bandiba, briefly per telephone on two occasions. He passed the conversations with flying colors. Admittedly their talk was in each case somewhat stilted because they knew their conversation was being monitored. They spoke each time mainly about family and children. Only one meeting was arranged between the new Bandiba and Binnie in the month before his release. He passed this physical meeting with Binnie with flying colors. They hugged briefly. They did not kiss. They spoke of each other's regard for one another and how they looked forward to the release and to being reunited.

At this meeting Binnie told him not to listen or take heed of rumors being spread about her. Belson had been briefed about her doings beforehand, so he said nothing. He had been told of her rise to leadership of the Youth Wing of the Black Congress, where she was a vehement advocate of violence and revolution. She supported "necklacing" of opponents, including those blacks who were in any way against the revolution. "Necklacing" was the term used for the placement of a motor car tire around the neck of the person being "necklaced" and then setting the tire alight so that the victim was burnt to death. He had been told of her liaisons with many men, some appointed by her to be her bodyguards, and of her liaisons with members of the soccer team she sponsored. He had also been told of charges supposedly soon to be brought against her for aiding and abetting the murder or manslaughter of a teenage boy called "Shorty" who had somehow angered or betrayed members of her soccer team.

Belson was told that it was important for him to pretend to ignore these matters. For his release to be a success, the outside world was to think that his marriage to Binnie was intact despite the many years of separation from her because of his incarceration.

Chapter 29

On February 11th 1990, as the day dawned upon South Africa, a new era dawned upon its inhabitants. Belson Bandiba was to be released. Thousands lined the route from the prison. Many thousands more waited in the hot sun of Cape Town's City Square, where he was to give his address to the nation. A great hullabaloo from press and media. World leaders and dignitaries, international movie stars and politicians from all over the world arrived in South Africa to be present in the country and of course to be seen associating themselves with this momentous event.

Belson's release was scheduled for 11.am, when he would be met by his wife Binnie outside the gate of the prison.

His release was delayed. This created an even more intense interest from the thousands awaiting the release. The delay was due to the presence of Belmond Fruttoo, who was the Anglican Archbishop of Cape Town. He was the first black man to be appointed to such an exalted rank. He insisted upon being allowed to see Belson before his release. Fruttoo was highly influential, not only due to his rank in the Anglican Church but also as a known stalwart of the Black African Congress. His insistence upon seeing Belson in private before his release had met with resistance from the authorities. He said he had come to give Belson Bandiba God's blessing. This was needed, he said, to ensure Bandiba's well being and the well being of the country. They allowed him to see Belson in private only when Prime Minister Van Blerk, to whom the request had been relayed, consented.

Van Blerk knew Archbishop Fruttoo as a "snake in the grass", one who, in the garb of a cleric had the deviousness of the devil. Or so Van Blerk categorized him. But Van Blerk was reluctant to offend Fruttoo. Of course, Van Blerk's very existence upon the earth offended Fruttoo. But Fruttoo was accustomed to get his way and would not consider backing down. He seldom backed down, always smiling, always saying he was there to do the will of God. In this matter he got his way once more.

Belson had been given the speech he was to make on his release by his minders. He had memorized it well and he could if needs be recite it backwards. So said his tutors. He did not need to refer to the written speech he had with him in order to recite it verbatim. Archbishop Fruttoo greeted him as effusively as he would have greeted his own brother. Indeed, he too had served time in prison for anti apartheid activities. They were brothers in race, brothers in the struggle against white oppression and brothers in religion. He insisted upon seeing the speech Belson had memorized. He read the speech. He then tore it up and gave Belson a speech which he and leading members of the Black National Congress had written and approved. Fruttoo had been searched before being allowed in to see Belson. However his bishop's mitre had not been removed or searched. In it he had secreted a speech which had been prepared and authorized by the leaders of the Black African Congress of which he was a leading light. Fruttoo himself had authored most of the speech.

He gave the speech to Belson. Fruttoo said "Belson,

you are my brother, my comrade, my friend, but you have been too long away from us. The speech you made is not what is needed for the struggle our people still have to continue against our oppressors. You must give this speech I have given you."

Belson said, "But what about my speech?" Fruttoo replied "You will say this speech now given you. This is an order from the leaders of the Black Congress."

Belson looked crestfallen, but he agreed.

"Oh, by the way, God bless you my comrade brother!" said Archbishop Fruttoo.

He adjusted his mitre and Belson, accompanied by Archbishop Fruttoo, went out of the prison gates, the head warder, two prison guards, and two South African security policemen with them. Hundreds of members of the press and media and a crowd of thousands awaited him.

Amidst cheers and cries of "Amandla,"which was the Xhosa word for power, he was kissed by a smiling Binnie Bandiba who was there to greet him and they walked hand in hand to face the crowds of well wishers and the barrage of photographers and the members of the news media. Mounting the podium on the makeshift platform, Belson gave the speech given him by Fruttoo:

"Friends, comrades and fellow South Africans. I greet you all in the name of peace, democracy and freedom for all.

I stand here before you not as a prophet but as a humble servant of you, the people.

I salute the Black National Congress.

I salute our President, Comrade Bolivar Bambo, for

leading the BNC even under the most difficult circumstances.

I salute the combatants of Umkonto e Assegai.

I salute the South African Communist Party."

He continued voicing the speech given him by Archbishop Fruttoo, which expressed sentiments in similar vein.

Chapter 30

Prime Minister Van Blerk had been watching Bandiba on television. He heard what Bandiba said in his speech. He was slowly getting apoplectic. He lost his temper. He called for his aide. Red in the face he screamt"What the fuck is this Kaffir saying? I will kick somebody's arse over this. Get me Retief," he ordered. Captain Retief had been in charge of the day to day conversion of Sipho to Bandiba. Retief came on the line. He was apologetic. "It must have been that bloody priest", he said, "Bandiba did not give the speech he was supposed to give!"

"I should cut Sipho's fucking balls off", Van Blerk yelled into the phone.

And that is what was done, or nearly done.

Belson Bandiba recited Archbishop Fruttoo's speech before the crowd of thousands. It was broadcast far and wide. All over the country, blacks, upon hearing the speech, raised their fists and yelled "Amandla." Indeed, the fiery words of the speech, his many references and thank you's to revolutionary supporters, were indicative of the move towards power by the black population of the country. At last their leader was free. And here he was saying things for which people would have been locked up only a few years ago. The black population vastly outnumbered the white population, but hade never been allowed to vote or share in the governance of South Africa.

Captain Retief spoke into the mouthpiece of his headset in the office where he had been watching the proceedings on a television monitor. He ordered Sipho to stop the speech, to feign illness, all to no avail. It appeared that Sipho had removed his earpiece. Retief said, "I'll bloody kill that Kaffir when I get my hands on him".

Captain Retief, on the orders of Prime Minister Van Blerk, did not kill Sipho. A week or so later, when the initial hullabaloo died down somewhat, the press was informed that Belson Bandiba was in need of rest, suffering from exhaustion. Bandiba was visited by a physician. The physician gave him an injection of a tranquilizer which effectively drugged him. Bandiba was taken by ambulance to a private clinic. Once awake and compos mentis, electrodes were applied to his testicles, causing him to feel pain as great as he had felt in the ritual circumcision he had undergone as a youth many years before. He was told that any future disobedience would result in worse torture, and if he wished to remain alive, he had better not disappoint his handlers again.

Again, Sipho weighed up his new found life of fame, luxury and good living, against the alternative of torture and death. And made his choice. He would continue his masquerade as Belson Bandiba. He would be obedient. If he disclosed his role in the impersonation of Belson Bandiba, he would be hated by his own people, and no doubt killed by the authorities.

He was then given an injection of Hypnoval and his unusual penile protuberance, which was the source of so much sexual satisfaction to him and his lady partners, was removed. At the same time a new small micro sized earpiece was implanted into his ear. This he would be unable to remove. Regarding the operation on his penis, he was told that it had to be done in case Binnie saw him naked. However he had not had sex with her and she did not press him for it. Sipho was not stupid. He saw the restoration of his penis to a normal shape by the removal of the source of so much pleasure to his sex partners as a punishment. But there was nothing he could do. He would remain Belson Bandiba. A docile Belson Bandiba, carrying out the orders of his masters. Bandiba was never seen without his earpiece again. The micro mini implant in his outer ear canal was there in case he removed his outer earpiece.

From that day on Belson Bandiba carried out the orders of his minders to the letter. He became an advocate of moderation. He spoke of peace. He advised caution and compromise. The adulation and reverence accorded him by the majority of the black population gave his words and opinions gravitas.

Only in the Province of Natal, home of the Zulu tribe, where Prince Bagisulo Fatulesi was the Chief, did he find opposition. Fatulesi wanted the lion's share in what was proposed regarding the future governance of South Africa. There were armed clashes between followers of Fatulesi, who were "Zulu Impi" and the followers of Bandiba, who were mainly Xhosa.

The white government, still entrenched in power, engaged in talks with Bandiba and Fatulesi regarding the implementation of universal suffrage for blacks as well as whites on a common electoral role. However, in the hope of delaying the ascension to power by the black majority, the white government clandestinely established and supported a mysterious "third force" which fomented armed clashes between the two opposing black factions. This "third force" was believed to have been created by the police themselves. Its members spread rumors and indulged in provocations in order to create clashes between the opposing factions. It secretly supplied weapons to both sides. The hope was that the blacks would ask the white government to remain in power for longer in order to maintain a modicum of peace in the country. Not all the clashes involved guns. In most clashes, traditional weapons such as "knob kerries" (fighting sticks), stones, bricks, and assegais (spears), were involved. However, some clashes involved the use of handguns and home made rifles as well as the clandestinely obtained automatic weapons. Lives were lost, heads bashed in, limbs broken. The country seemed to be on the verge of chaos. The white government was not asked to step in to maintain order.

Bandiba advocated peace and power sharing. This was because Van Blerk had by now realized that there was no way to avoid complete collapse and widespread internecine warfare in South Africa without power sharing by all factions, black as well as white. He had Bandiba as his puppet, and Bandiba helped in the accomplishment of this task. Bandiba advocated restraint, forgiveness and tolerance

There were hiccups. Some whites were reluctant to give up power. One Fergene Berblanche, a charismatic white man, who lead a right wing faction of white supremacists, proposed succession from South Africa and the formation of an independent "all white country" to be called "Oranjia" within South Africa. They attacked and shot at blacks and even fired at the South African Police, who made some attempt at restraining them.

After many meetings and discussions with the leaders of various factions, elections were held. For the first time the black population, many of them illiterate, voted. Thousands stood for hours in the blazing sun, lining patiently in lines stretching for hundreds of yards, in towns and rural districts in order to cast their vote. There were long ballot papers with pictures in the party colors and photographs of the many candidates to enable the illiterate to make their choice.

International election monitors were present to oversee the election process. Naïve and prone to wishful thinking, the monitors gave the election their approval. However, as with many elections in Africa, the whole process was a farce. Ballot boxes were lost. These votes and many others were not counted. Voters were bussed in to vote, many voted more than once. The dead voted. In view of the general hullaballoo and expectation surrounding the election, it would have not have been possible to declare the election a farce. There had to be a result. The contenders met to discuss this. They negotiated the result. They took the decision, in secret of course, to announce the result of the election, as though the voters had decided it.

The results were announced, giving the Black National Congress a majority, with the White National Party close behind. The Independent Zulu Party was accorded some presence. So also, a small Democratic white party.

The world was happy, most South Africans were happy. Van Blerk was, in the circumstances relatively happy. Belson Bandiba, who was installed as State President of the new South Africa, was very happy. He now had status, respect, and a life of luxury and wealth. Belson knew, however, that if he put one foot wrong, he would be subjected to horrible fate, for the reach of the Covert Operation Division of the old Intelligence Agency, still heavily influenced and run by whites, was long.

CHAPTER 31

Willem Wasson, of the South African National Intelligence Agency had many titles. He was the de facto Head of Covert Operations.

He ordered a flight by an Atlas Rooivalk helicopter. Two passengers boarded. Rather they were "helped" aboard by Covert Agency personnel for they were heavily drugged. The helicopter flew over the river in Mpumalanga which formed the Southern border of the Kruger National Park. The river was called "The Crocodile River" for obvious reasons.

The helicopter returned to base without the two passengers. They had been bundled out and dropped into the river.

Willem Wasson, who arranged this, felt the irony of the Crocodile River being used. The Prime Minister, M.W. Motha, colloquially called "Die Groot Krokodil," (The Big Crocodile) had given him the orders during his premiership. "When the time comes, get rid of Sipho's wife Beauty and Belson Bandiba." "The time will be when the new Belson is released to the world. Drop them into the Crocodile River."

The new Prime Minister, S. B. Van Blerk, when asked by Wasson to confirm this instruction had said "Willem, I know nothing of this. You have been given your orders. Carry them out. You must always carry out orders. But remember what I say. I know nothing of this order. I deny ever speaking to you in this connection."

After the crocodiles did their work, no trace was left.

Chapter 32
December 1993.

Belson Bandiba, now President of South Africa and Leader of the Black African Congress and S.B.Van Blerk, former Prime Minister of South Africa, attend the Nobel Awards Ceremony in Oslo, Norway, to receive their Nobel Peace Prize awards.

The fact that South Africa was hardly peaceful did not seam to concern the Nobel Prize Awards Committee.

In his acceptance speech Belson congratulated his former "nemesis" S.B. Van Blerk. The speech he made had of course been written for him by his handlers, on the order of S.B.Van Blerk.

S.B.Van Blerk, in his acceptance speech spoke of peace, yet admitted that in the year 1993, three thousand people had lost their lives due to political violence. He did not give figures for crime related to black on black violence associated with robbery, rape and arson, or the figures for crime and injuries and death for black on white crime related to theft, robbery and rape.

At the awards ceremony mention was made of Archbishop Fruttoo, who had previously been awarded the Nobel Peace Prize. He too was widely honored and respected world wide.

It was Van Berk, who was heard to say "Well done, Sipho" after the ceremony. Onlookers thought Sipho was a nickname Van Blerk used for Belson Bandiba. Van

Blerk now seemed to use it every time he spoke privately to Belson Bandiba.

Belson, who had been made President of South Africa, was awarded numerous honorary degrees, both in South Africa and worldwide. Statues were erected in his honor in overseas countries. Streets, schools and housing developments in countries as far afield as England were named after him. Kings and Queens received him. He welcomed the likes of Yasser Arafat and Colonel Gaddafi to his audience. Movie stars, pop singers, posed with him. Multi millionaires as well as the impoverished sought his audience and his council and advice. This was often given. It consisted in the main of platitudes. He had no compunction saying to his secretary "Get me the Pope", and lo and behold, the Pope was on the line. "Get me the President of France" and lo and behold Jacque Chirac came on the line.

In April 1996, Belson Bandiba, aged seventy seven years, was granted a divorce from Binnie Bandiba, then aged sixty one years, on the grounds that she was unfaithful. Belson had hoped for an amicable settlement, but true to form, Binnie did not go quietly. She made much of how she sustained her husband by her stalwart support during his twenty seven years of incarceration and by keeping her faith and activities in the Black African Congress.

Bandiba was prepared to negotiate a settlement out of court, but she wanted the equivalent of five million dollars. Bandiba said that he had instructed his lawyers to negotiate an ex gratia payment to her and a waiver of costs granted by the courts in his favor. She refused. She then failed to appear in court.

Bandiba was granted the divorce. He said "I am glad that the case is over and regret that my ex-wife cannot bring herself to negotiate an amicable settlement. He said he was suspicious that his wife was committing adultery and that her unfaithfulness was confirmed when he saw a love letter she had written to her personal assistant, a lawyer by name Bani Mapuma. Her unfaithfulness over the years was widely known, including her dalliances with her bodyguards and members of her soccer team. Binnie, of course, denied this. She had indulged in much profligate spending and was also accused of fraud in several matters.

Belson was now free to take another wife.

Belson's popularity continued unabated even after the divorce. Some considered that the Pope be asked to confer Sainthood upon him. Only his being alive seemed to mitigate against this.

Binnie Bandiba, hardly a saint, was put on trial after many delays and postponements for the murder of "Shorty" but evaded sentencing, and remained a free woman, still active in the Black African Congress.

CHAPTER 33

Sipho Bondiswa continues his life as Belson Bandiba. Now an old man, retired from the presidency, he is somewhat senile, but is still sufficiently receptive and welcoming of adulation. He revels in the role of greatness accorded him and has in his own mind become Belson Bandiba.

He took a new wife, a woman called Bracca, who formerly was the wife of the black president of a neighboring country. She remains a gracious lady, unlike the divorced Binnie, wife of the real Belson, and unlike Beauty, Sipho's real spouse, who he never saw or heard of again after he became Belson Bandiba.

Many ironies abound in the story of South Africa and future historians will be left to contemplate the many co-incidences therein. One of these is that Bracca became a widow and therefore eligible to marry Belson when her first husband, Bamora Bachel, who was president of Mozambique, died in a plane crash. The cause of the crash remains uncertain but was thought to be the result of covert action by persons or agencies unknown. It was rumored that decoy aircraft radio beacons had lured the aircraft to its crash site and that South African agents were involved. Motha and Van Blerk denied any hand in this tragic event. However, it would seem that the new Belson met her and became enamored of her before the plane crash. The truth surrounding the airplane crash has not come out. However, Bamora Bachel's death in the air crash suited both the South African government and the new Belson Bandiba.

Bracca Bandiba may be the only woman to have been the wife of two presidents of two different countries.

The crowning irony was the establishment of a Truth and Reconciliation Commission in South Africa. The new Belson Bandiba and Archbishop Fruttoo, headed this body, which was composed of eminent jurists as well as prominent political and well known personalities. Those who suffered in the apartheid days and those who caused the suffering were brought before the commission which had the power to impose sentences or dispense forgiveness. Truth from both the accusers and the accused was sought. It was hoped that those who perpetrated the offences would come clean and that those who suffered at their hands would find it in their hearts to forgive. The new Belson Bandiba headed the commission.

M.W. Motha, by then retired, cocked a snoot at the Truth and Reconciliation Commission. He refused to appear before the Commission. He called it a circus.

S. B. Van Blerk, however, did appear before the Commission. He denied that he ever had knowledge of or that he had ordered atrocities. He was never sentenced.

It is thought that Van Blerk, or his covert agents, still handle the new Belson. The new Belson, has been made aware that should his role in replacing the true Belson become known, he would be torn to shreds by his adulating followers.

Binnie Bandiba appeared before the Commission. Although forty witnesses gave evidence implicating her in various crimes, including being associated with murder, she denied all charges. The witnesses were motivated by malice towards her or were liars, she said. She received no sentence and remains a free woman, although she lost her position as leader of the Black Congress Youth Wing and her position as a Member of Parliament of South Africa.

Willem Wasson appeared before the Commission. The charges against him were many. His case was a long one. He was acquitted. He was later charged in criminal court with dealing and possession of a large amount of "Ecstasy" tablets. He was also acquitted on this charge, which was miniscule in comparison to the charges he faced before the Truth and Reconciliation Commission.

During his appearance before the Truth and Reconciliation Commission he was dubbed "Dr. Death" by the media. He spent thirty months in the dock. On being acquitted he commented that the forty million rand (four million dollars) spent by the state on his prosecution could have been better spent paying for and providing the anti AIDS drug Nevirapine to HIV positive pregnant mothers. The irony here was that this statement came from the man who was rumored to have been instrumental in the initial spread of the disease. Allegations in regard to spread of the HIV or AIDS never came before the Commission or the Courts.

There was evidence led that he was head of "Operation Coast" the apartheid government's secret biological and chemical warfare program. Testimony placed before the Truth and Reconciliation Commission by witnesses related to a host of bizarre and grotesque killing methods. "Operation Coast" attempted to produce a range of "smart" poisons which would only affect blacks. Cholera and anthrax was hoarded in vast quantities which could cause major epidemics. Weapons researched included chocolates containing the botulism poison. Sugar was laced with salmonella. Whisky was laced with herbicide. Beer with drugs producing infertility. Cigarettes were laced with anthrax.

Experiments were done using naked black men who were tied to trees and then painted with poisonous gels. Any survivors were killed with muscle relaxants.

Captain Retief was never brought before the Truth and Reconciliation Commission. He was appointed to the highest post given a white person in a group known as "The Scorpions", a new elite squad appointed by the new government to investigate and root out corruption and crime in the country.

It soon developed the reputation of being corrupt itself. It was subsequently disbanded.

The Truth and Reconciliation Commission was indeed a circus. The chairperson or head was nominally the new Belson. Archbishop Fruttoo, was the de facto head. He was the Clown in Chief. The others, in trying to appear dignified and solemnly judicial, looked just as comical.

Most of the sentences were farcical. The really guilty were acquitted. Some of the guilty received unheard of severe sentences. One Eugene De Blok, who was alleged to have committed many atrocities and who admitted to most of them, was sentenced to two hundred and twelve years in prison. This ridiculous sentence further confirmed the farcical nature of the costly exercise of the "Truth and Reconciliation Commission"

Many considered the Commission with derision. When Binnie Bandiba was called to appear before the

Commission, she arrived in a black Mercedes car, with the number plate 666NBB GP. This would have cost quite a considerable sum, as special number plates in Johannesburg were expensive to acquire. NBB were her initials, 666 was the symbol of the anti Christ. GP stood for Gauteng Province, although it was jokingly called "Gangster's Province" Her docket number 358/11/88 disappeared. Charges relating to" necklacing" were never brought. She was acquitted.

The Commission did nothing of real import to establish truth and reconciliation. The country of South Africa, once the example of all that was best in the African Continent, is now known for its ever increasing crime rate, the continued poverty of the majority of its newly enfranchised masses and the corruption of its government, its police and its judicial system.

Belson Bandiba is retired now. He is still accorded the adulation of the world at large and most of the black population of South Africa.

Sipho Bandiswa as Belson Bandiba continues to act out the role of Belson Bandiba, albeit in retirement.

He is no longer alert and tends to doze off at functions. He is dragged about by the Black National Congress stalwarts so that his presence can lend support to the party, which having failed to deliver most of its promises needs his presence. He is somewhat like a blow up doll propped up besides the driver of car in where more than one person is needed in the vehicle to qualify for driving in the lane. He is now over ninety one years of age, often forgetful and appearing to be near dotage. This helps his continued masquerade, as the public is inclined to forgive an old man his lapses. He recently tried to institute legal action against a Belgravia art gallery in London which was auctioning some of his signed artwork he was supposed to have made in prison. He denied having signed these works, despite witnesses coming forward to say they were present when he signed the works in the 1960's. Of course Sipho did not sign the works. The real Belson Bandiba did. Lapses like this are to be expected from an old man, or so most think.

Awards, accolades and honorary degrees continue to be bestowed on him. Some admirers have implored the Catholic Church to consider him for Sainthood.

Only one award, that of the "Oscar," the one he truly deserves for playing Belson Bandiba on the world stage, has not been given him.

The national anthem of the new South Africa is "N'kosi Sikkel iAfrika--God Bless Africa". Nowadays it certainly needs God's blessing.

Nkosi Sikelel iAfrika - God Bless Africa

Lord, bless Africa
Let its name be praised
(May her horn rise high up)
Listen also to our pleas
Lord bless
Us thy children
Come spirit
(come spirit and bless us)
Come spirit
Come spirit holy spirit
And bless Us, Us thy children

Lord Bless our Nation
And end all conflicts,
O bless our nation.
 Nkosi Sikelel iAfrika

Nkosi sikelel' iAfrika
Maluphakamis' uphondo lwayo
Yizwa imithandazo yethu
Usisikelele, usisikele

Nkosi Sikelel' iAfrika
Maluphakmis' uphondo lwayo
Yizwa imithandazo yethu
Nkosi sikelela, Thina lusapho Iwayo

Woza Moya (woza, woza)
Woza Moya, oyingcwele
Nkosi sikelela
Thina lusapho lwayo

Morena boloka Sechaba sa heso
O fedise dintwa le matswenyeho
Morena boloka sechaba sa heso
O fedise dintwa le matswenyeho

O se boloke, o se boloke
O se boloke, o se boloke
Sechaba sa heso, Sechaba sa heso
O se boloke Morena, o se boloke
O se boloke Sechaba, o se boloke
Sechaba sa heso, se Sechaba sa heso

Ma kube njalo! Ma kube njalo!
Kude kube ngunaphakade
Kude kube ngunaphakade!

Die Stem van Suid-Afrika

Uit die blou van one hemel, uit die diepte van ons
    see,
Oor ons ewige gebergtes waar die kranse antwoord
    gee,
Deur ons ver-verlate vlaktes met die kreun van
    ossewa -
Ruis die stem van ons geliefde, van ons land Suid-
    Afrika.

Ons sal antwoord op jou roepstem, ons sal offer wat
    jy vra:
Ons sal lewe, ons sal sterwe - ons vir jou, Suid-Afrika

In die merg van ons gebeente, in ons hart en siel en
    gees,
In ons roem op ons verlede, in ons hoop of wat sal
    wees,
In ons wil en werk en wandel, van ons wieg tot aan
    ons graf -
Deel geen ander land ons liefde, trek geen ander trou
    ons af.

Vaderland! ons sal die adel van jou naam met ere dra:
Waar en trou as Afrikaners - kinders van Suid-Afrika.

In die songloed van ons somer, in ons winternag se
    kou,
In die lente van ons liefde, in die lanfer van ons rou,
By die klink van huweliks-klokkies, by die kluitklap
    op die kis -
Streel jou stem ons nooit verniet nie, weet jy waar jou
    kinders is.
Op jou roep se ons nooit nee nie, se ons altyd, altyd
    ja:
Om te lewe, om te sterwe - ja, ons kom Suid-Afrika.

Op U Almag vas vertrouend het ons vadere gebou:
Skenk ook ons die krag, o Here! om te handhaaf en
    te hou -
Dat die erwe van ons vad're vir ons kinders erwe bly:
Knegte van die Allerhoogste, teen die hele wereld vry.

Soos ons vadere vertrou het, leer ook ons vertrou, o
    Heer -
Met ons land en met ons nasie sal dit wel wees, God
    regeer.

The Call of South Africa

Ringing out from our blue heavens, from our deep
    seas breaking round;
Over everlasting mountains where the echoing crags
    resound;
From our plains where creaking wagons cut their
    trails into the earth -
Calls the spirit of our Country, of the land that gave
    us birth.

At thy call we shall not falter, firm and steadfast we
    shall stand,
At thy will to live or perish, O South Africa, dear
    land.

In our body and our spirit, in our inmost heart held
    fast;
in the promise of our future and the glory of our
    past;
In our will, our work, our striving, from the cradle to
    the grave -
There's no land that shares our loving, and no bond
    that can enslave.

Thou hast borne us and we know thee. May our
    deeds to all proclaim
Our enduring love and service to thy honour and thy
    name.

In the golden warmth of summer, in the chill of
    winter's air,
in the surging life of springtime, in the autumn of
    despair;
When the wedding bells are chiming or when those
    we love do depart;
Thou dost know us for thy children and dost take us
    to thy heart.

Loudly peals the answering chorus; We are thine, and
    we shall stand,
Be it life or death, to answer to thy call, beloved land.

In thy power, Almighty, trusting, did our fathers
    build of old;
Strengthen then, O Lord, their children to defend, to
    love, to hold -
That the heritage they gave us for our children yet
    may be;
Bondsmen only of the Highest and before the whole
    world free.

As our fathers trusted humbly, teach us, Lord, to
    trust Thee still;
Guard our land and guide our people in Thy way to
    do Thy will.